FOR JUST CLAWS

KAREN ROSE WILSON

© 2002 by Karen Rose Wilson. All rights reserved.

No part of this book may be reproduced, stored in a retrieval system, or transmitted by any means, electronic, mechanical, photocopying, recording, or otherwise, without written permission from the author.

ISBN: 0-7596-8067-1

This book is printed on acid free paper.

1stBooks - rev. 01/29/02

ACKNOWLEDGMENTS

Thanks to Tracy and Karen for help with police routine; to Don, for giving me somewhere to type; to Edith; to Peggy for the first draft; to Pete for his patience as messenger; and to my veterinarian, Karl, for his advice. Thanks also to my sister, Rita, for the early revisions and encouragement; to everyone in the Borders group, especially John and Jana; to Patty; and, of course, to Jack who isn't Jack and Denise who isn't Denise.

AUTHOR'S NOTE

This is a work of fiction. All character's names and actions are entirely imaginary. Although the small towns of Hadley and Ortonville do exist in Southeastern Michigan, any resemblance any character may have to an actual person living or working there is purely coincidental.

PROLOGUE

Our small town of Hadley, nestled in the rolling green hills of lower Michigan, is normally pretty quiet. We ride our horses, pay our bills and sometimes forget to lock our doors. Murder and mercy killing, robbery and street protests are distant evils, things we read about in the Sunday newspaper, published forty miles away in Detroit, and brought by truck in the middle of the night.

All that was about to change.

CHAPTER ONE

I swung my lead rope and clucked to the two chestnuts eyeing me suspiciously from the corner of the paddock. I worked them, sending them swerving and turning, controlling their movements, outside turn, inside turn, herding them into the barn. Their hooves flung clods of black April muck, as they trotted to their stalls and I threw home latches behind them. The phone in the tack room sent me racing, counting the rings before the answering machine in the house picked up.

"What time are we saddling up?"

Puffing from the run, I glanced at my watch. "Hi Denise. I just brought the horses in. Feather's a real pigsty, mud from stem to stern." I fiddled with a balled-up spider carcass lying on the window ledge, rolling it between my fingers. "Grooming her isn't going to be quick. Let's meet in the meadow, at, say, half past twelve?"

"Great. I can't go for a long ride, got to be home by two. Todd and I are leaving for the hospital at three."

"How's his mom doing?" I asked, dropping the spider into the trash can.

"The cancer is taking over, day by day. Nothing will stop it now. We feel so helpless."

"How's Todd taking it?"

"We have these awful silences, when I ask him about things, like her will or her funeral, and he answers in a single word, then he doesn't want to talk anymore."

"Give him time, he'll come around."

"Time is the one thing we don't have. Somebody's got to talk to her about the important stuff. Does she want to be cremated or buried? Life support or not? But no, they talk about trivial things, like the weather or who won the baseball game."

"It hasn't sunken in yet. What's obvious to us, I mean. He's still denying that she's dying."

"He knows the truth, just as sure as you and I."

Feather fidgeted on the cross-ties, shifted her weight, and cocked her right hind heel. "Not to change the subject, but I've got housecleaning and grocery shopping on today's agenda, so I can't go for a long ride either."

"Sounds good. See ya' later."

I curried and brushed my mare, picked out her feet and combed her mane and tail. Stretchy neoprene wraps went on to protect her legs and support old, worn tendons.

Her stablemate, Echo, poked his head over his Dutch door and yawned. "Tomorrow's your turn," I reminded him. "Feather goes today and you go tomorrow." He shook his head, flapping his tongue against the stall door.

Closing the paddock gate behind us, I led Feather across the lawn and stood on the picnic table, positioning the mare alongside, to slide my foot into the stirrup. We ambled down the gravel road, sun peeking through cottony clouds and a warm breeze ruffling last autumn's damp leaves. The dirty snow had melted, giving way to spring flowers crowning moist earth.

I tapped my heels against Feather's sides and we trotted onto a path that wound around some honeysuckle bushes and opened into a meadow. Following a narrow deer trail through the meadow, this was a shortcut that saved riding up a steep, rocky hill on the gravel road. Lemon-yellow sulphurs flitted among the yet unfurled honeysuckle buds.

Feather's ears twitched forward and back, listening. We scrambled over the rubble of an old stone wall and stepped onto a two-track left by hunters, rutted with the deep gouges of four-wheel drives. A hundred feet to the south, the two-track dead-ended into the county road.

Denise and I usually met along this stretch, where the land is state owned and posted as equestrian trails and, during hunting season, open to hunters. I closed my legs around Feather's sides, almost imperceptibly released the reins, and we broke into a canter, her steel horseshoes rhythmically clicking on the stony path. Rounding a curve, Denise rode toward us.

She pulled up her gelding, Beezer, and turned him, so he and Feather walked side by side. "Like your hair," I said. She'd gotten it done since I last saw her. "Nice highlights." Her brown eyes, fringed in dark downcast lashes, gave her a coy princess charm.

"I stopped by Jill's salon Thursday after work," she said. "She did my hair while I looked at pictures of her new filly." She pulled a pack of cigarettes from her denim jacket and lit one. The smoke curled and spiraled upward, like spirits rising to heaven.

"Having a sister that's a hair stylist definitely has its perks. What's the new horse like?" I asked.

"It's not a yearling, like she wanted. She ended up getting a two-year-old through one of her trainers."

"A two-year-old is better anyway. She won't have to pour as much time and money into her before she's rideable."

"The down side is that she had to pay more than she expected."

"Looks like she'll need a few more of those hundred-dollars-a-cut customers to help pay the bills." We were at a fork in the two-track. "Which way?" I asked.

"Let's take Blood Road, go through the pines and up the big hill to the overlook." She pulled an old prescription bottle from her pocket, pinched the end of her cigarette butt, and dropped it into the bottle. "How'd they ever come up with a name like Blood Road?" she asked.

"You never heard the rumor? Way back when we were in high school?"

She shook her head. "I wasn't raised around here, remember? I was a city girl."

"Yeah, I always forget." She seemed so at ease in the country, with her horses and dogs and chickens, I always forgot she was transplanted. "Well, the story was that couples came out here to park or party, drink beer, whatever. With it being so desolate, no houses and all, it was a popular spot. Supposedly a couple stopped to park but left their radio playing. When they wanted to go home, the battery was drained and the car wouldn't start, so he said he would walk to the nearest house for help. He told her to lock all the doors and not to let anybody in, except him. Sometime in the night, she fell asleep, but dreamed she heard a tapping noise."

"And no doubt it was a stormy, moonless night," Denise said skeptically.

"Of course," I said. "When the sun came up, she found the source of the tapping—her boyfriend hung from a tree, a noose around his neck, his shoes tapping the driver's side window."

She threw me a crooked grin and tucked a lock of hair behind her ear. "You believe that?" she asked.

"Of course not," I laughed. "But that's why it's called Blood Road." The road was sandy and straight here, perfect for a short gallop. "Let's canter," I called to her.

Feather surged forward when I drew back my leg and laid my heel against her side. The wind whistled past. At Blood Road, we slowed to a walk and turned right, then took a path leading to a stand of towering Tamarack pines so dense and dark and foreboding that even on the brightest day, only a blue-green streak of light passed through to the forest floor. Silent except for the crunch of hooves on fallen pine needles and creaking saddle leather, the pine forest was a mystical vacuum cut off from the rest of the world.

We went up a steep hill, where erosion exposed the gnarled roots of the tall pines. The horses carefully picked their way over the roots, some as thick and strong as woven nylon rope. At the top of the hill, out of the shadows of the Tamaracks, welcome sunlight streamed down again. The horses puffed from the long climb.

"Oh, I almost forgot to tell you," said Denise, "remember Kathy's son, Derrick? He's come back to live with her."

"As if she doesn't have enough to do—the only ranger managing a four-thousand acre state park—now she's got him to look after, too." Less than thrilled to hear he was in the neighborhood, I said, "Nail down everything that moves and board up your house."

"Carol, give the kid a chance. He's been gone three years."

"In the first place, he's not a kid. He must be seventeen by now. And in the second place, you know Kathy only sent him to live with his dad in Detroit because she couldn't do a thing with him. And I hate to generalize, but Detroit hasn't been voted best community to raise children in lately, so I doubt he's improved."

"She says he's grown up a lot. Some of the bad things he did were just part of being a kid."

"So being a kid gives free license to be a kleptomaniac?"

"Would you want to be judged the rest of your life on what you did as a teenager? Give him another chance, even if just for Kathy's sake."

"Let's say I'm not ready to have him house-sit while Jack and I go on vacation."

"Honestly, Carol, you'd be suspicious of Noah, if it was raining and he offered you a lift in his Ark."

"I'm not that bad, I'm just realistic. I can't help it; it comes from living with Jack." Husbands are easily blamed for shortcomings. I figured he had it coming, since it was his cynical nature rubbing off on me.

After climbing the last ridge to the overlook, we let the horses snack on grass while Denise and I dangled our feet out of our stirrups. We could see far to the south, over the tops of the trees, and all the way to the water tower fifteen miles away.

"Guess I'd better head home," Denise said. "Wish I could ride longer."

"Me too. You know how weekends are—errands, laundry, housecleaning, grocery shopping. It's always a mad rush to catch up, like fitting your entire life into two days a week."

"The hectic life of a working woman," she said. "Want to ride tomorrow if it doesn't rain?"

"Sure. Around one o'clock?"

"It'll be Echo's turn." I always reminded her when I brought Echo, my problem horse. Last fall, he grabbed Beezer's bridle and pulled it off his head, breaking the bridle in the process. Denise rode home with a polo wrap fashioned into a makeshift headstall. Another time, he bit Beezer's knee. A third time he took hold of Beezer's tail and yanked it, starting a kicking spree that ended with Denise face down in the dust.

"We'll just stay far enough apart so he can't get into mischief," she said.

"You're so good natured about his naughtiness. I don't think I'd be as charitable."

"He's just playful. And it's not like he's ever done any real damage. You've got to let them have their personalities, Carol, just like kids."

"He's got a personality, all right—a bad one. A thousand pounds of juvenile delinquent, with poor vision and the mentality of a scared rabbit."

She laughed. "You're too hard on him. It's a good thing you never had kids. They wouldn't have ever had any fun."

"At least they wouldn't be total brats, either, like most kids nowadays. They aren't taught any respect, the way *we* were."

"This is a discussion for another day, Carol Ward, you old fogey." She smiled. "I've got to go."

"Just cut me off, mid-sentence, that's okay," I complained. "No respect for your elders." Denise was exactly six months younger than me.

CHAPTER TWO

The sun was low by the time I turned my truck into Marge Butler's drive. Bailey Boo, her twelve-year-old collie, lifted his head from the porch step and opened clouded eyes, sniffing the air. Good old Bailey Boo couldn't see a thing, except maybe shadows.

The green aluminum-sided split-level was sheltered from the road by a group of large pine trees. To the right and behind the house stood a green pole barn, where Roy Butler's well-drilling equipment had been stored. The business had been sold, along with the equipment, when he died five years ago.

I banged my knuckles hard on the aluminum screen door to get Marge's attention. She pulled the inner wooden door open and I saw her weathered face break into a smile.

"Carolyn, good afternoon!" she chirped, like I had just set the universe aglow.

Thinking someone actually enjoyed seeing me that much made me smile. "Hi Marge. Got everything on your list this week, except the Cheerios. They were out. Said they'd have more Monday, I can get them for you then, if you'd like."

"Don't worry, I've got plenty of corn flakes. You do enough, getting my groceries every Saturday, like you do.

I just wish you'd let me pay you for your trouble." She pulled the loops of one of the plastic bags from my wrist.

"It's no trouble. I'm going to the supermarket anyway, what's the bother picking up a few extra things?"

Her white hair, tinged slightly blue, was neatly curled, as if she had simply slid the curling iron out of each curl, leaving it intact, and sprayed it with lacquer. Dressed in a navy-blue flowered tunic and beige polyester slacks with taupe crepe-soled shoes, she led me into the kitchen.

"The half-gallon milk was on sale, so I got it instead of your usual quart. I hope that's okay."

"Sure is. I can always use some extra calcium."

"I think we all could. By the way, the clothing drive is next Sunday. Did you want to donate anything?" By anything, I meant Roy's old clothes.

"I've got the bags all ready to go, in the living room."

The house had the musty, closed-up smell of old mothballs, but there wasn't a speck of dust to be found. Cotton doilies lay across the headrests of the easy chairs. Mahogany woodwork bordered willow-green walls and carpeting the color of creamy eggnog. Bailey Boo's plaid cedar-filled bed lay in front of the hearth.

Her eyes darted to the bags on the floor. "I've gone through everything. It took me all week, believe it or not. I'd cry a little, and have to sit down for a cup of tea. Then, when I felt better, I'd go back to it again. Little by little, I got it done."

"I'm sorry, Marge, I should have offered to help. How thoughtless of me."

"Oh, no mind. It was the kind of thing one has to do alone. I looked at something, remembered how he looked wearing it, remembered when I bought it for him, remembered his favorite things, his not-so-favorite things.

Then I'd remember how much I miss him." She toyed with the gold locket she wore around her neck. "I'm not sure I would have been good company; and you've got so much, working all day and taking care of all those animals, you don't have the time to fuss with an old lady like me."

"Don't be silly. You know the saying, 'If you're too busy for friends, you're just plain too busy.'"

She pointed to the bags on the floor. "Well, there they are. Let me help you get these out to your truck."

She pulled a gray wool sweater from the top of one of the bags. "On second thought, I know someone who would love a nice warm sweater like this. I'm surprised I didn't think of him sooner." She held it up, as if sizing it. Roy's initials were monogrammed in black thread, the three letters forming a diamond.

"It's a beautiful sweater," I agreed.

Bailey Boo tagged along as we carried the bags out to my truck. I set them down on the passenger side floor, got in the driver's side, and rolled down the window. "Let me know if you need anything. And don't be afraid to ask Wolfman Jack, either. He doesn't bite, he just looks like a hairy beast. Judging by the hours he spends in front of the television, he's got loads of free time."

She laughed. "The things you girls say about your husbands these days!"

"I'm afraid they've fallen off their pedestals," I yelled out the window, heading down the drive.

Jack sat in a patio chair on the deck, unlacing his work boots. "The back door wasn't locked."

Here we go again. "I was only gone a few minutes, just to deliver Marge's groceries."

"I want you to lock up when you leave the house."

"Look around you, Jack, who do you see? It's just us. We live in the country, remember?"

He slid the patio door open. "I don't care. Just lock the doors, okay?"

"Yeah, sure," I mumbled. He was right, I knew. Especially now that Derrick was back.

CHAPTER THREE

A bushy tail swiped back and forth, like a metronome, across my face. Cat hairs danced and floated in the beam of sunlight streaming through the open blinds. Maximillian, an obese coon cat, sat on my pillow, and three more felines slept at the foot of the bed: Angelic white Camille, black as night Imp, and golden-eyed Boots. Hannibal, my beloved schizophrenic, who, in a split second changes from a sweet, sensible lap cat to a fangs barred, claws unsheathed, demon, slept on the chair across from my bed. Obviously brother and sister, with almost identical black and white coats, Boots and Hannibal came as a package deal last year, found crouched near my mailbox, in what Jack believes was a perfectly orchestrated drop-off.

I've scheduled an appointment for Hannibal with a kitty psychiatrist, but *aggressive behavior*, his receptionist informs me, *is absolutely rampant*, and the good doctor is so overbooked, he can't fit us in until next month. Now to find a way to justify cat psychiatry, on our meager budget, when Jack balances the checkbook.

An early riser, wide awake the instant his eyes opened, Jack sat on the couch reading the Sunday paper and sipping coffee. "Hannibal left three headless mice on the door mat."

"Wonder why he eats only the heads?" I asked, pouring myself a cup of coffee.

"Because he's a psycho cat."

I warmed my hands around the mug. "What'd you do with them?" I asked.

"Nothing. I left them for you, since he's your cat. Front page or sales ads? I know you don't want the sports section," he said.

"Neither. I've got to feed." The horses stood at the gate, voracious eyes focused on the house, waiting for the moment the patio door slid open, and, amid fervent nickering, I emerged. So involved was I in my daydream, that I jumped when the phone rang.

"Yeah, she just rolled out of bed. Hang on." Jack held the phone out, "It's Denise."

"What's up?"

"Kathy just called. Do you know Rene's daughter?"

"Julie? Sure." If it weren't for the row of blue spruce along our driveway, I could see the back of their barn. "She feeds my horses and cleans my stalls when we're out of town. Why?"

"She needed a tape-recording of bird songs for her college biology class, so she hiked into the park yesterday afternoon and she's still not back. Rene's worried sick that she's lost."

"How could she be lost?" I asked. "She's ridden those trails as many times as you or I."

"I don't think she's lost," Denise continued. "After dark, Rene called Kathy and told her Julie still wasn't back and the two of them went looking for her. But by then they couldn't see a thing, so Rene called the police. Two officers came out, looked around the house and barn, asked a lot of questions and then drove through the park. Nobody's seen hide nor hair of her."

"What about her girlfriends? Maybe she spent the night at a friend's house."

"They called her friends. None of them know a thing."

"No wonder Rene's sick with worry," I said. I ran my fingers nervously through my uncombed hair, tugging at the ends.

"The police suggested she's simply left home without telling Rene, but that's ridiculous. She loves that horse of hers. She wouldn't leave Cinders and not say a word to Rene."

"Julie's got more sense than that," I said. Jack's startled eyes lifted above the newspaper. "This is really strange. What if she's sprained an ankle or broken her leg and can't walk home? She's probably terrified after a night alone in the woods, not to mention cold and hungry. Why didn't someone call us last night to look for her? We know those trails like the backs of our hands."

"The police searched all night. They're bringing in the K-9 Unit from Oakland County right now. Call it intuition or ESP or whatever you want, but I'm getting a funny feeling about this. Why don't you and I saddle up and help look? They don't want Rene to leave the house in case Julie calls or shows up."

I looked at the wall clock, calculating time. "I haven't fed the horses yet, but I can be saddled up by half past nine."

"We can meet on Fox Lake Road, then split up and meet back on Blood Road, by the sand hills. That'll cover the main trail. If we still haven't found her, we can decide which way to go after that."

I hung up the phone. "What's going on?" Jack asked. "Where's Julie?"

"Good question. She's been gone since yesterday afternoon."

He folded back the front page of the sports section. "She take her horse?"

"No. Denise says she hiked into the park to tape-record songbirds for a college science project and that's the last anyone's seen of her. Poor kid, it's spooky out there at night." I thought of Denise's premonition.

He looked at his watch. "I'd better get going. Tom and I are running the store by ourselves today."

"We're going to have a look. We were going riding anyway, we'll just split up and cover different trails."

"Don't go stickin' your nose in where you're not wanted. The police have plenty on their hands as it is, without you two making matters worse."

Pulling on my jacket, I said, "It can't hurt to look."

Down at the barn, I scooped oats into Feather and Echo's buckets, then packed their hayracks and filled the water tank before heading up to the house.

Jack gave me a quick kiss on his way out the door, as I was coming in. "I hope we've found her by the time you're home from work," I said.

"I hope so, too. Gotta' go. Don't make a nuisance of yourself with the police, okay? The last thing they need right now is Lucy Ricardo and Ethel Mertz interfering."

A muddy field boot sailed through the air, but my timing was off, and all it hit was the back of the door.

CHAPTER FOUR

I heaved the heavy western saddle onto Echo's back and pulled the cinch tight. In my cantle bag, I stuffed a couple elastic bandages and an extra sweater, along with a bottle of water and a sandwich. I swung into the saddle and fifteen minutes later met Denise on Beezer, waiting by the stop sign at the end of the road. Her cupped hands sheltered a cigarette she tried to light, unsuccessfully, in the wind. "Maybe somebody up above's hinting you should quit smoking." I said.

"Very funny, Miss Ward."

I was *Miss* when she was ticked off. The rest of the time I was Carol. "We'll meet at the crossing of the sand hills?" I asked.

"Yeah, sure. What time?"

I pulled back my sleeve to glance at my watch. "Ten-thirty?"

She turned Beezer back in the direction she came from and trotted off.

April sun filtered through leafy green boughs and fell on clusters of trilliums. The woods were beautiful this time of year. Up ahead, two uniformed officers walked, radios clipped to their belts. Startled by the clicking of Echo's horseshoes on the stony trail when I rode up behind them, they turned around.

"The lost girl is my neighbor," I said. "Has she been found?"

"No ma'am. Not a sign."

"This park covers thousands of acres, and that's just the bridle paths," I said.

"Don't worry, ma'am, if she's here, the dogs'll find her."

At ten-thirty, I was at our rendezvous point. Denise cantered toward me, coming out of a curve in the sandy road. "See anything?" she called.

"Only two police officers west of Jossman Road. How about you?"

"Not a thing."

"Where to next?" I asked.

"We could check the pine forest," she said. "If we split up now, I'll go through the swamp and come in from the south side. If you start here, we'll meet in the middle."

Following the same trail I'd taken the day before with Feather, the massive Tamaracks swayed, creaking and groaning in the wind. Suddenly Echo jerked his head up high and whirled around, nearly throwing me, and bolted in the direction of home. For a moment I was unbalanced, hanging over his left side, and when I regained my seat, I brought him to a halt.

"Settle down, fella," I told him, trying to calm myself at the same time. His neck trembled under my hand. Figuring the wind had him spooked, I spurred him forward, but he snorted and stopped abruptly, in the same spot where he pulled the first about-face. A deer carcass lay in the trail ahead, in the murky shadows of the pines.

Anchored to the ground, wild-eyed and snorting and puffing, Echo refused to move until I kicked him again, this time harder, and he leapt forward. Then he backed up so fast we lost the forward ground we'd gained. I was afraid that if he whirled around again I'd get dumped for sure, so, with shaking hands, I dismounted to lead him past the deer.

When I got closer, I wished I'd let him bolt for home. It wasn't a deer—it was Julie.

A huge hole gaped through her chest. Mangled flesh and dried blood commingled with threads of the shredded jacket she wore. Fine yellow pollen from the trees had blown into her eyes, which were locked, wide open, in a frozen stare. One arm was raised over her head, like a rag doll flung down on the floor.

A sickening heaviness gripped my stomach, doubling me over. A deafening sound, like the blaring whistle of a freight train, rang in my ears. Turning my head away, I sank to my knees, gasping for air. I crouched with my head down, one shaking hand on the ground, the other holding the reins, until everything stopped swaying.

Something rustled in the bushes, a chipmunk or a squirrel, and Echo pulled violently backward, jerking the reins in my hand. "Dammit," I yelled, "Get a grip!" Jack was right. I shouldn't have butted in where I didn't belong. I should have let someone else find her.

Denise rode into the clearing. "What's wrong? I heard yelling." Her eyes shifted downward. "Oh, my God, what happened?" She jumped off Beezer and ran toward me, Beezer trotting behind. "What happened?" she screamed.

I tried to tell her, but I was sure she couldn't hear me. "It's Julie. She's been shot." She stood in horror, looking down. I could not steady my trembling hands. "One of us has to stay here and one of us has to find the police." Echo rolled his eyes, the whites showing, as he snorted and pulled backward again.

"I'll go," Denise said. She looked awfully pale.

"Hurry. I don't know how much longer I can hold Echo. He knows something's wrong. These reins are going to break if he keeps jerking on them."

She was crying. Our faces met, her dark eyes locking on mine. "Who would do this?"

I didn't answer.

"The troopers you saw earlier, where were they?" she asked.

I pointed the way up the path. "Stay on this trail where it crosses Blood Road, go up into the sand hills, and keep heading east. It's still morning, so the sun is in the east. Just keep riding toward the sun and you should catch up to them. Go, before I change my mind about staying."

She nodded, climbed up on Beezer, and was gone.

Cold sweat crept down my back. I thought about Denise's question. Who did this? And why? Could it have been a hunting accident? Maybe a poacher mistakenly shot Julie and, afraid of the consequences, abandoned her. But Julie had been gone since yesterday afternoon. Poaching was generally a nighttime activity. Jack would know what hunting, if any, was open this time of the year. I wished desperately that he was with me now.

Then I remembered why Julie was out here. Where was her tape recorder? Had her murderer taken it? I didn't touch Julie or disturb anything around her, knowing the police would want everything left exactly as I'd found it. A sharp wind blew through the pines. I shivered in their towering darkness, praying Denise hurried.

It was past noon when I rode across my lawn and led Echo into the paddock. Thirty-five years of horse ownership gave me the ability to groom on automatic pilot, because while my hands worked, my mind relived the scene in the woods. I could not stop seeing Julie's mangled flesh or stop hearing the crunch of pine needles under my feet when I knelt by her side.

Echo's coat was matted with dried sweat, so I hosed him down and threw a wool cooler over him, then turned him loose to graze in the backyard. Feather stood patiently at the gate, waiting for me to halter her and let her out, too.

I called the lumberyard and let the phone ring. "Hi, it's me," I said when Jack picked up. When I heard his voice, I couldn't hold back the tears any longer.

"Did Echo buck you off again?" Jack asked quickly. "That horse has got to go!"

"It's not Echo," I sobbed.

"What then?"

"I found Julie."

"And?" He waited. "Is she back home?"

She was home all right. "Jack, she's *dead*."

"Dead? How can she be dead? What happened?"

"She's been shot. It was unbelievable, the front of her was just gone, *blown away!*"

"Take a deep breath," Jack said. "Now, start over. Did you get the police?"

"Well, *of course* we got the police," I sniffed. "Denise went for them while I stayed with Julie."

"I figured it was a simple misunderstanding, I really did, that she'd gone to a friend's house and forgot to tell her mom." He sounded dazed.

"I keep thinking it's a bad dream, and I'll be so relieved when I wake up, because I never would have known what to do if it had been real. But this *is* real," I said. Someone called Jack's name. "I know you're busy, I'll go. When will you be home?"

"In about an hour. Have a shot of whiskey; it'll do you good."

"Whiskey is not a cure-all, Jack." I laid the phone down and blew my nose.

Keeping an eye on the horses from the dining room window, I looked for something to eat, then decided I wasn't hungry after all. The jar of peanut butter, on the counter where I'd left it this morning, reminded me of the sandwich still in my saddle bag.

Julie had eaten an entire jar of extra crunchy peanut butter when she house-sat for us last summer. It seemed so long ago, almost in another lifetime.

Tears rolled down my cheeks. I held the bottle of Jim Beam in one hand and thinking, just this once, maybe Jack was right, I poured a glass and took it out to the deck, sinking into a lounge chair.

Almost two hours had passed since I found her. I thought of Rene and how alone she must feel. Julie was an only child, whose dad left years ago for a job on the west coast. Rene rarely heard from him.

Sheltered by the house from the wind, the deck was warm in the afternoon sun. My eyes felt heavy. The fragrance of lily of the valley, growing on the north side of the house, seemed overpowering. In a dream it smothered me, like a warm, wet blanket over my face. A truck door slammed and I sat straight up with a start.

Jack's voice boomed. "The horses are in Lyle's apple orchard again! Traipsing all over the neighbor's property, doing whatever they damn well please!"

They must have shimmied under the makeshift clothesline fence, because the horses were on a feeding frenzy of last year's rotted windfall. Apple slime drooled down their chins and dripped to the ground in frothy pools. I wondered how long they'd been there, praying they hadn't eaten enough apples to colic.

"Get home!" I shrieked and pointed toward the barn. Off they charged, bucking and kicking, clods of Lyle's soggy lawn flying from their hooves. They slid under the clothesline, leaving six-foot skid marks, then cavorted and frolicked while I frantically herded them toward the gate, yelling and waving my arms. Feather snorted and gave one last leap on her way into the paddock. A hoof-shaped disk of mud flew from her heels, and walloped me in the face. I slammed the gate shut.

Jack shook his head. "It's less than four weeks until Lyle gets back from Florida. I'm not taking the fall for this—they're your horses, not mine."

"He's *never* back before Memorial Day," I retorted. "It'll be as good as new by then. And Lyle's not picky about how his lawn looks anyway."

"That doesn't mean he wants a cavalry charging across it."

It took me an hour to fill in the potholes, replacing chunks of sod, tamping the dirt down and smoothing it out. The horses watched innocently from the gate.

When I got up to the house, a fleet of roaring cars, covered in bright advertisements, wove in and out on the television screen. In some warm southern locale, spectators wore sleeveless shirts and sun hats at a Sunday afternoon stock car race.

Pulling off muddy boots, I left them on the sisal mat. "Lyle's lawn is fixed."

"I don't understand why you can't keep your horses locked up."

"They beg to go out, it's their reward for good behavior."

"What good behavior?"

"If I hadn't taken your suggestion, I wouldn't have fallen asleep. 'Have a shot of whiskey, Carol, it'll do you good.'"

He reached out for my hand. "You just sounded so upset on the phone, it was all I could think of. Feeling better now?" he asked.

"I don't know," I said, slumping into a chair. Instantly Camille was on my lap. She circled, kneading her toes, then finally plopped down. Stroking the underside of her throat, I felt the soft vibration of her purr. "I feel so empty, but that's not even the right word, so futile, like everything's so futile. Life in general. Like you just wake up one day and, bam, you're dead."

"Carol, if you're dead, you don't wake up."

"Don't be a smart ass. You know what I mean. Do you always have to be so literal?"

"Look at it this way—there's not a thing either one of us can do to bring her back, so why wish for things that aren't going to happen? Wishing never changed anything. It just uses up a whole lot of time and energy."

"In a warped sort of way, I suppose that makes sense." Was this a bad sign? Had my sanity been compromised by too many years with Jack? "It just doesn't seem right to go about our daily business, like nothing's happened."

"Don't you think I'd bring her back in an instant if I could? She was a good kid. Too young to die." He pointed the remote, and the whining tires fell into the background. "You never gave me details."

"There's not a whole lot to tell. After the police came, they wanted Denise and I out of the way. Detectives poured in like an army on maneuvers. Yellow tape strung from tree to tree; radios blasted; it was like a scene from Columbo. Echo was a nervous wreck, jigging and prancing, and I was too tired to fight with him, so I came home. I imagine the reporters have swarmed in by now, at least the ones with four-wheel drives, anyway. A sheriff's car was out front at Rene's."

"I don't envy that job," Jack said, "Giving someone that kind of news." He reached to pull a wisp of hay out of my hair.

"By the way, what kind of hunting is open now?" I asked.

"Is somebody trying to pin this on a hunter?"

"No, I just wondered."

"There's rabbit and squirrel just about all the time and raccoon at night. And it might be turkey season." He pulled open the bottom drawer of the coffee table and, rifling through a sheaf of papers, found the Michigan Department of Natural Resources hunting guide. He flipped through it, found the page, and said, "Turkey's open."

"Could she have been killed by a turkey hunter?" I asked. "Don't they use buckshot for turkeys, same as for pheasant?"

"It's called turkey load, a shell with about ten big BBs. One of them could kill somebody if it was close enough."

"But would it blow a hole right through a person?"

"I'd doubt it."

"This whole thing is sickening. We're talking about Julie, our neighbor, not a statistic in a study on firearms. I can't believe we're even discussing it," I said.

It was late Sunday afternoon when I rang Denise. "Heard anything more?" I asked.

"Kathy called about an hour ago. The sheriff broke the news to Rene. They've taken Julie for autopsy, but it looks like gunshot wound was the cause of death. Ron, Julie's dad, is on his way from California. Derrick is manning the phone at the ranger station so Kathy can stay with Rene tonight."

"Anything we can do to help?"

"I've got a casserole baking that I was going to drop off for Rene and Kathy's dinner. I can meet you over there in about an hour and we can feed the horses and muck stalls. Maybe hang around a little and see if they need us for anything."

"I'll bring a salad to go with the casserole," I said.

I chopped carrots, celery, onion and potatoes, then cubed a pound of stew beef, and threw it into a crock pot with a can of beef stock. I tossed a salad, packed it up, and, standing at the patio door, said to Jack, "I'm taking a salad over to Rene's. I'll be back in a couple hours." He tore his eyes from the car race only long enough to nod. "I've left a pot of stew simmering for our dinner."

I worried over what I would say to Rene, but I shouldn't have, because when she answered the door, and I looked into her eyes, my heart went out to her. I wrapped my arms around her and held her and we both cried.

"My baby. My baby's gone," she sobbed. "How will I live without her? Who would do this?"

"We'll find out," I said. *Don't make promises you can't keep, Carol. You haven't a clue as to how to find Julie's killer.*

In the foyer, behind Rene, stood Kathy, whose natural attractiveness always amazed me, even now. Her shoulder-length blond hair, thick bangs and big brown eyes gave her an effortless, outdoorsy look, like the women in L.L. Bean ads.

Denise said, "We thought we'd help with barn chores. We can feed, water, clean stalls, whatever."

"Anything would be great," Kathy answered. She led us into the kitchen. "We're glad you stopped by, the sheriff wants a word with you."

The sheriff sat at the table, surrounded by papers, pens and half-filled styrofoam coffee cups. Guessing him to be early fifties, he was paunchy, with sparse salt and pepper hair.

"Sheriff Morton, the two ladies who found Julie are here. I'm going to take Rene upstairs."

He turned to face us. "We've got a homicide on our hands," he said slowly, as if searching carefully for each word.

"Homicide?" I blurted. "What about a hunting accident? Isn't it turkey season?" Somehow an accident seemed easier to swallow.

"Without an autopsy report, anything I say is just my opinion, mind you, but I do *not* believe this was an accident. The bullet wound suggests a higher caliber than that used for small game or turkey and the location of the body, in an area of clear sight, precludes an accidental shooting. The lowest branches on those pines are twelve feet up, twice the height of a man, easily.

I'm told Julie was carrying a tape recorder, and after search, it hasn't been found. The *knowledge* of the recorder's existence is of extreme importance to this case."

I understood the implications. Voices, sounds, the sequence of the entire murder itself, could be recorded on that tape. But where was it?

He continued, "Other than police officers, and, of course, the killer, you ladies are the only persons who saw the victim. Think carefully of who you've spoken with since the body was found, to whom the tape recording may have been mentioned."

I swallowed hard. I never asked Jack not to mention Julie's death to anyone. "I talked to my husband, but he was at work; he may have told someone else."

Denise said, "Same here—I told my husband. He spent all morning plowing up our garden and then went to the hospital to see his mother. I doubt he's said anything to anyone, except maybe his mom."

The sheriff pushed a pad of notepaper toward us. "I'll need both of your full names and addresses and to speak with your husbands as soon as possible. It's crucial that no one else hears of the tape recorder. *Do not* pass any additional information on to *anyone* until you've heard further from me."

I wondered if his pallor was the result of too many hours spent sitting behind a desk. I asked, "But if it wasn't an accident, and she was murdered, then there must be a motive, right? What possible reason could anyone have for killing Julie? She was just a kid." Somewhere in the house a clock chimed six times.

"That's what we aim to find out. Are your husbands home now? Might I stop by to talk with each of them?"

I considered Jack's irritability, coupled with his general distrust of law enforcement personnel, and answered, "My husband would *love* to talk to you, stop by any time."

Yeah, right. When pigs fly.

CHAPTER FIVE

"How'd it go with the sheriff?" I set soup plates, silverware and glasses on the table.

"Thanks a lot for sending him over without warning. Just who I wanted to see on a Sunday afternoon, while I'm having a beer and watching the car race."

"As far as I know, there's no law against drinking beer in your own home, so it wasn't like you had anything to hide, and besides, it was urgent he talk to you. Had you told anyone about the tape recorder?"

"You've got to be kidding! We were so busy, I never even got a chance to eat my lunch. Damned weekend do-it-yourselfers."

"Did you know you are an incessant complainer? The cats are a nuisance; the horses make a mess; the damned do-it-yourselfers. It's one thing right after another." I set the soup tureen on the table and went back to the kitchen for a ladle and napkins.

"Camille just swished her tail through the stew! Can't you do something with these cats?"

"What do you suggest, Jack?"

"For starters, why can't they stay outside, where they belong?"

"Be my guest. You be the ogre who throws them out, then watches them lick the patio door, begging to be let in from the cold."

"Cold, my ass. It's at least fifty degrees out there!"

As if fifty degrees was a heat wave.

After shooing Camille from my chair, I ladled out two bowls of stew. Max and Imp leapt from chair to chair, playing tag. Suddenly Max jumped onto the table, one gigantic hairy paw landing in my stew. He flew down the hallway, shaking stew with every step.

My blood pressure soared. Jack was, for once, shocked into silence. Picking up his soup plate, he went into the living room, from which, at a decibel level high enough to wake the dead, came the opening theme of a Bonanza rerun.

Jack drinks. I take bubble baths. I slammed the bathroom door and turned on the hot water, full blast.

CHAPTER SIX

Five-fifteen, Monday morning. Exactly one hour and forty-five minutes stood between me and a thirty-mile trek to my job. But first, quality time with my cats. Max climbed aboard my stomach, his echoing purr begging forgiveness for last night's faux pas. Idly scratching his ears, I thought of Sheriff Morton's words. *We've got a homicide on our hands.*

People are murdered every day in nearby Detroit, and not always for a reason. But this wasn't Detroit. This is a sleepy farm community an hour's drive north. What if some weirdo drove up from the city for the day, killed Julie, and sped back? But that was just plain absurd! If they wanted the satisfaction of bumping someone off, they could have stayed home and done that. Nothing made sense.

I microwaved a bowl of oatmeal and ate it while I watched The Weather Channel. Rain was forecasted for the whole day and, though it wasn't daylight yet, what I could see looked dismal. Fat rain drops hit with a splat, then streamed down the glass door wall. Didn't look like I'd be doing any riding today, which was just as well. I had errands to run on the way home from work.

Jack stumbled into the kitchen. "Can I ride in with you today? My truck doesn't run worth beans when it's damp." He ran his fingers through tousled sandy-brown hair.

"When are you going to change those ancient spark plugs?" I asked. It was a rhetorical question. "Be ready to go by seven." Carpooling was a simple matter, since the lumberyard was along my route. "I'm heading down to the barn to feed, we can leave right after that."

Rain fell steadily, like a lace veil cascading over hills and fields. The horizon was a monochromatic study in Payne's gray, promising a day that hovered between predawn and twilight, with little difference in-between.

Low nickers in the darkness answered my morning greeting to the horses. Impatient for his breakfast, Echo shook his head and pawed the air, as if counting, with his hoof. Thinking I'd throw him a couple flakes of hay before getting grain buckets, I realized I'd forgotten to throw hay down from the loft last night.

The second-story loft was separated into three rooms by a creaky wooden stairway, one room to each side of the stairs, with windows facing west, and the largest room straight ahead. The light switch was at the top of the stairs, so I picked my way slowly up the dark steps, all the while holding my breath and imagining icy fingers on the back of my neck. Hay was piled into two stacks, four bales high, with a walkway through the middle. A trap door opened into a stall down below and another larger door opened to the outside of the barn, a sheer drop of twenty feet.

I quickly threw two bales down the trap door, turned off the light, and had my foot on the first step when I thought I heard a low moan. *Don't be silly*, I told myself, it's just the weathervane, creaking in the wind. Then I heard it again. Stepping into the small room to my right, the toe of my boot rammed against something in the doorway. Something I knew shouldn't be there. Something soft.

Terrified, I flew down the stairs, tripped on the last one and sprawled headfirst onto the landing. Panicked by the noise of my fall, the horses charged out of the barn, their steel-shod hooves clattering down the asphalt aisle. I tried to scream Jack's name, but with the wind knocked out of me, nothing came out except a wheeze. Gasping painfully, my lungs filled to bursting, and I ran, screaming, up to the house.

"Jack! There's something in the loft! It made a noise like a moan, and when I tried to see what it was, my foot caught on something, whatever it was, and it was dark and I couldn't see, but I felt it move!"

"It's probably the wind, blowing in under the eaves."

"It is *not* the wind. I touched it, whatever it was, I told you, it was soft and it moved!"

"What do you want me to do about it?" he asked.

"Go see what it is!"

"Carol, we're going to be late for work."

"I don't give a damn! Something's in the hayloft and I'm not going anywhere until I know what it is."

Grabbing a flashlight, he said, "Okay, fine. To make you happy, we'll scare all the big, bad spooks away." He pulled his revolver down from the closet shelf.

"Well, for God's sake, what do you need that for? We're not going to shoot anybody are we?"

"Just in case."

"In case of what?"

"Just in case. Let's go."

He strode out the door, across the lawn and straight up the stairs, without a moment's hesitation. At six-foot-four, two hundred pounds, and carrying a gun, I guess there wasn't much Jack had to be afraid of. I stayed on the landing, listening to the horses pace back and forth in the paddock, mud squishing under their hooves.

Jack flicked on the light at the top of the stairs. "Holy shit!" He kneeled, setting the revolver on the floor. "Call 911! Tell them we need an ambulance. Hurry! And throw me a horse blanket, Feather's turnout rug, anything, to wrap him in."

"Wrap who?"

"Just call 911! Now! And get the blankets."

I made the call, then grabbed Feather's wool cooler from the wall rack and ran up the steps. "They're on the way. Shouldn't be long."

Sprawled on the floor, an old man shivered in a rain-soaked gray sweater and ragged jeans. Gray stubble covered his face, a face I'd seen before. But that wasn't why I stood taken aback in silence.

Jack looked up. "Know him?" he asked.

"Yeah. He camps down by Algoe Lake. Sometimes he's wandering along the lake, or picking pop cans by the road. Whew! Judging by a whiff of him, I'd say he drinks a bit. Funny, I didn't notice that smell earlier."

"You probably weren't close enough. Must have crawled up here, trying to get in out of the rain. Nothin' but skin and bones. Might be in shock."

Jack wrapped the blue plaid cooler around the old guy, tucking the edges underneath, like a cocoon, then brushed stringy gray hair away from his face and told him it was all right, don't worry, the ambulance was on its way. I ran downstairs for more horse blankets.

I'd seen more than just his face before. He was wearing the sweater Marge changed her mind about donating. The one with Roy's diamond-shaped monogram on the front.

Jack told the paramedics we'd found him, soaked to the bone and nearly unconscious, in our hayloft. I added that I'd seen him before, camping over by the lake.

"I called work and told Lora I'd be in late."

"I hope he makes it," Jack said. He pulled taut the laces of his leather work boots. "If we stop and get a newspaper, we'll know what's been reported about Julie. That way, we won't slip and say something we shouldn't."

Fifteen minutes later, we picked up the Tri-County Gazette at a party store on the main highway just outside of town. Hitting rush hour's tail-end, I wove in and out in the pouring rain, while Jack read me a capsulized version of the front-page article.

"A young woman, who had been hiking in a nearby state park, was reported missing in the early evening hours on Saturday. She was found dead Sunday morning, on one of the park's remote bridle paths, a victim of a gunshot wound. Investigation pending."

"That's it?" I asked. "A kid gets killed and all she gets is a lousy paragraph?"

"Basically. And two pictures—her senior picture and one with Cinders. She's holding a trophy." He folded the newspaper and held it up for me to see.

"County Fair, two years ago," I said. "She won Equitation over Fences in her division."

"So all we can say is that she was our neighbor and somebody shot her. Pretty sketchy." A rusty truck pulled out of a side street, causing the car in front of me to skid on the wet pavement. "Thank God for anti-lock brakes," I said. "What about the old man? What do we say about him?" *And how the heck did he get Roy Butler's sweater?*

"I don't think he's got anything to do with Julie. I think he was sick or drunk or both and crawled into our loft to get out of the weather. He probably makes the rounds of all the barns in the area. No one locks barn doors; it would be easy to slip inside, after dark."

"It gives me the willies to think he's been up there before, maybe at times when I was down in the feed room, and I didn't know. I think I'll call the hospital later today to check on him."

Jack slid the newspaper into the door pocket. "I don't recall you mentioning a homeless person."

"I didn't say I *knew* he was homeless. I said I'd seen him down by the lake. A lot of people camp down there and it doesn't mean they're homeless."

"Yeah, but do they camp in *April*, for God's sake? It's not summertime. He isn't even wearing a coat."

"I never paid attention; it just seemed like I saw him every now and then. I never gave him a second thought." Splashing into the puddled parking lot, I stopped at the lumberyard gate. "Working until five?"

"As far as I know. If anything changes, I'll call you before you leave work."

"Five on the nose, then. We've got a couple stops to make on the way home."

I still had a long way to go. Windshield wipers methodically swiped away drizzle as rain-soaked miles passed. Traffic thinned through the grimy, industrial section of Pontiac, where they manufactured cars and trucks. Like any large city, it had more than its fair share of crime. I took my chances, I knew, by taking this route, but it cut a good ten minutes off my drive.

The change was dramatic when, in a few short miles, Pontiac gave way to affluent Bloomfield Hills. Beautiful homes sat, like modern-day castles, on acres of manicured lawns. Maids and chauffeurs began morning rituals. I slipped into the underground parking structure, then took the elevator to the marble-floored commons area, where four law firms were nestled behind doors with shining brass name plates.

I was exactly one hour late. The aroma of freshly-brewed coffee pulled me like a magnet to the kitchen, where Lora arranged china cups on a silver tray. Her short black hair accentuated her narrow chiseled face and ice-blue eyes.

"Morning," she smiled. "What's going on? You were positively cryptic on the phone."

"For starters, some old geezer collapsed in our hayloft. We called 911 and they've taken him to the hospital, but that's not all. Did you hear about the body found in the state park?" I didn't wait for an answer. "She's my neighbor," I said, realizing I'd just referred to Julie in the present tense.

She reached for the crystal cream set. "How awful! Did you know her well?"

"She took care of my animals last summer when Jack and I went on vacation and she mows our lawn. We've ridden together a few times. A nice kid; real outdoorsy."

"How'd it happen?"

Lora's question jolted me. The one I dreaded answering. But before I got a word out, Chet and David, bemoaning the succumbing of the Tigers to San Francisco, passed the kitchen without noticing us. I used the diversion to duck the question. "They missed their calling," I said, "they should have been baseball coaches instead of lawyers."

The morning passed quickly. Chet was going to Dallas tomorrow to close a land deal, and as usual, he'd waited until the last minute to get his typing done. I could have used two more hands and a couple extra hours.

On my lunch hour I phoned the hospital and, after explaining who I was and what I wanted and being put on hold three times, was finally connected with the patient services administrator. A woman who spoke sparingly, as if sentences were sold by the word, simply said, "No identification and no known relatives, might as well tell you."

"Tell me what?" I asked.

"Died. Poisoned."

"Poisoned!" I was flabbergasted.

"Autopsy will tell. Lab's running more tests. Ambulance driver gave your name and address as ID. Been trying to get a hold of you."

Her sentence fragments were getting on my nerves. "I'm at work," I said.

"Sheriff wants a word with you."

Not again. I needed to talk to Marge first, to ask her about the sweater. "I'll give you my work number. I'm here until four."

I rang Jack immediately. "John Doe didn't make it. And now they think he was poisoned."

"Poisoned! What kind of poison?"

"They're running more conclusive tests right now."

"If we'd only found him sooner, maybe we could have saved him."

"The sheriff wants to talk to us *again*." I watched the second hand sweep around the face of my desk clock. "And, Jack, there's something else. Something I didn't tell you this morning."

"Good God, Carol, what else can there be? Yesterday you find the neighbor girl dead, today it's a semi-comatose wino. What next?"

I ignored the innuendo. "The sweater he was wearing, the one with the monogram?"

"Yeah? What about it?"

"It was Roy Butler's sweater. Marge pulled it out of a bag of clothes she was donating to the church clothing drive. Last Saturday, when I dropped off her groceries, we were loading up the clothing bags, and she said she remembered someone who'd want the sweater. I'm positive it was the same one, there's no mistaking that monogram. What am I going to do? The sheriff is sure to ask me if I know anything about the monogram. I can't lie, but if I tell him the truth, it'll point a finger at Marge."

"Marge Butler wouldn't hurt a fly, let alone poison someone."

"I know that, and you know that."

"And why on earth would she off an old hobo?"

"I'm not saying she poisoned him, I just don't want to send the sheriff over there, snooping around, asking a lot of questions and making her nervous. She's my friend and I won't do that to her if I can help it."

Chet came around the corner of my cubicle with a document. Jabbing his finger at the pages, he mouthed instructions which I neither heard nor understood, but shook my head affirmatively to, hoping I'd figure it out later. "Got to go," I said to Jack, and hung up.

With telephone cradled between neck and shoulder, typing furiously, I rang Marge a few minutes later. "Marge? Hi, it's Carol." I forged ahead. "Say, Marge, last Saturday, when I picked up your clothing donation, and you pulled that gray sweater out—I hope you don't mind my asking, but what did you do with it?"

Without a moment's hesitation, she answered, "I gave it to the old man who lives in the park—well, he doesn't exactly *live* in the park, he lives with his daughter in town most of the time. But he hits the sauce a bit, and the daughter doesn't like that, so he camps out in the park when he's drinking. Why?"

Sounded like she knew him pretty well. "Jack and I found him in our barn this morning, soaking wet and nearly unconscious. We called 911 but he died a couple hours later, at the hospital."

"Good Lord! Oh dear, this is awful, Carol. He was such a nice fellow, he'd never hurt anybody."

"The hospital said he had no ID. Do you know his name, or his daughter's name, so she can be notified?"

"I only knew him as Randy. Yes, I imagine someone should tell his daughter, but the only thing I know about her is that she lives in town. This is awful, just awful, I can't believe it. Yesterday that darling little Julie and today Randy. I just don't know what things are coming to, Carol, honestly, I just don't know." She paused before asking, "What did he die from?"

"He may have been poisoned. Autopsy report will tell for sure."

"Poisoned?" Marge's voice seemed strangely far away and small.

I wondered if we'd lost our connection, and waited for what seemed an eternity. "Marge? Hello? Are you there?"

Her voice trembled. "Carol, you'll have to excuse me. I'm not feeling well. I think I'll lie down."

I was dying to know Marge's connection to Randy. Thankfully, the sheriff hadn't called, and though I wasn't sure I wanted to point him in Marge's direction, she was hiding something, of that I was certain, by the way she clammed up when I mentioned the word poison.

At four o'clock I did my best to make some order of my desk, mostly by opening my top desk drawer and shoving everything in, helter skelter, to be dealt with tomorrow. Ginny, our receptionist, had one ear glued to the phone, so I signed out at the front desk and waved good-bye.

Thick clouds hung low, like a soggy gray quilt. I decided to take the expressway, not only to save time, but hoping to see my red-tailed hawk. Half-way between work and home, sometimes he perched in an old gray oak tree near the side of the road. Other times I watched him glide, then swoop and dive. I imagined what it would be like to fly, how the wind would slide over my outstretched wings. There was no sign of him today, either in the heavy wet air or the tree.

It wasn't five yet, so I waited for Jack at the lumberyard, listening to the radio, until I saw him locking up, his canvas jacket slung across one shoulder.

"So how many court battles were won today?" he asked, throwing his jacket in first.

"I keep telling you, Chet is not a litigator." His mountainous frame filled the compact truck. "I called Marge after I talked to you and I'm sure she knows something. Something she didn't want to tell me." The truck sank into a pothole and mud splashed the windshield. "By the way, the old fella's name is Randy. I got that much out of her before she feigned not feeling well to get me off the phone. At the beginning of our conversation she felt fine, then, as soon as I mentioned poison, she suddenly took sick and had to hang up."

"Doesn't sound like Marge," he said. He turned away, looking out at the rain. "Maybe you shouldn't ride alone in the woods until this is cleared up."

"Until what's cleared up?" I asked.

He turned to me, his face somber. "There've been two murders in two days' time."

"You said yourself you didn't think the old man had anything to do with Julie."

"That was before we knew he was poisoned. It would only be temporary, until things settle down."

I switched the radio off. "Denise works weekdays from ten to six; she rides first thing in the morning, before work. I have to ride in the evening, *after* work. There's no other time and there isn't anyone else to ride with."

"What about the people at the quarter horse farm?" he asked.

"You've got to be kidding, Jack! They never set foot out of the indoor arena."

"Ask them if you can ride inside, too."

"The indoor ring is for boarders only. There's this whole etiquette thing, passing inside shoulder to outside hand, or the other way around, I don't remember. I gave all that up when I stopped showing. Besides, going around in circles isn't my cup of tea anymore."

He jutted his chin out, the cords in his neck bulging. "Then don't ride at all."

Lots of women let their husbands dictate to them, but I wasn't about to become one. "Who do you think you are, making a demand like that?"

"I'm not demanding, I'm asking. Can't you do something for me, just because I asked?"

"No, I can't, Jack." How could I make him understand the magnitude of what he wanted? "Riding is my only freedom, it's *my* time, when everything else falls away. Please don't make this an issue."

"It's you who is making it an issue, not me!"

We were stopped at a red light. I looked into his eyes, at the flecks of yellow and gray. "Maybe you shouldn't deer hunt anymore. It's dangerous. Every year men are accidentally shot or die of heart attacks, dragging a carcass out of the woods."

"That's different." He sullenly turned back to the window.

We drove in an uneasy silence into town. "Can you take the truck and go to the granary, while I get groceries, then come back for me?" I pretended the argument never happened, wishing it away, as if it had been imagined.

"Yeah, sure. What do you need?" he asked.

"A hundred pounds of pellets and a hundred pounds of sweet feed. And a sack of Calf Manna." I fished in my purse, watching the road from the corner of my eye, and passed my wallet to Jack. "Take about fifty bucks."

I tore a deposit slip from my checkbook and handed it to him, along with a pencil. "Write it down. A hundred pounds of pellets, a hundred pounds of sweet feed, fifty pounds of Calf Manna."

He had the archaic and disgusting habit of licking the end of the lead pencil before writing. It reminded me of our milkman, thirty-five years ago, taking my mother's dairy order.

"How do you spell manna?" he asked.

God, please give me strength. "M-A-N-N-A," I answered.

"That's not how they spelled it in the Bible."

"I don't care how they spelled it in the Bible. That's the way the company spells it. What does it matter how it's spelled, anyway? Just say 'Calf Manna' to Betty, she'll know what you mean."

"Yes, oh great and powerful Oz."

Fuming, I took a perverse pleasure in seeing his head snap forward when I slammed on the brakes in front of the supermarket. Today was strictly speed shopping, no idle label-reading or price comparison. Jack would be back within twenty minutes.

As I careened around the soft drink aisle, into frozen foods, I spotted Dr. Adler, the small animal veterinarian, shuffling toward me. If he saw the cheap grocery store-brand cat food in my cart, I'd be in for the full forty-five minute discussion on the pitfalls of high ash and magnesium feline diets. I knew the whole spiel, practically by heart, and it wasn't that I didn't believe him, because I did, it was just that today I didn't have either the time or the patience for it. I opened the nearest locker and heaped frozen dinners strategically around and over the cat food, burying it.

His cart slid up to mine. "Carol, hello!" He shoved his glasses up on his nose. "How are all my little patients this sodden, dismal day?"

"Oh, just fine, just fine." Conversations with Dr. Adler needed very little incentive to become lengthy. Middle-aged, tall and thin, lumps of dishwater blond mop stuck out on both sides of his ears, giving him a mad scientist look. I was used to seeing him in his wrinkled lab coat with his name embroidered in red thread on the pocket.

There was no time for visiting, especially with the frozen dinners unthawing in my cart, so I gave him my best smile and scurried past him on my way to the checkouts. He called out from behind me, almost as if he'd been struck with an afterthought, "That poor girl, the one who died in the woods, that wasn't too far from your place, was it?"

I turned around, but still inched my cart forward. "Just down the road."

"What's the world coming to, anyway?"

I could see we were headed toward a long discussion of the general disrepair of the universe, so I politely said, "My husband's waiting; I'd better get going. I think Camille is due for her shots next month. See you then."

He smiled and looked at me with that faraway look of his, as if I was already long forgotten and he had moved on to the theory of relativity or some other equally important revelation of mankind.

The ride home was a quiet one. I shuttled groceries from the truck to the porch, and Jack carried the feed to the barn. It was raining hard.

What awaited me in the house came as a total shock. I left my keys dangling from the front door and raced to the back of the house. "Jack!" I yelled, "Our house has been broken into!"

He dropped the bag of pellets inside the barn and slammed the door closed. Like a football player he ran, full of power and might and hulk, across the wet lawn.

The rocking chair was overturned. Jack's stuffed ring-neck pheasant, now only a Styrofoam core, had been knocked from the shelf, its iridescent feathers strewn about. My beautiful philodendron, given to me by my mother as a cutting, and which I so lovingly nurtured, lay wilted on the floor, its ceramic dish shattered. Paw prints tracked dirt from the dining room, down the hall. One of the litter pans was overturned, and cat litter was in the carpet, on the chairs, flung into bookshelves along the wall.

"This was no robbery," Jack said, his finger sweeping the room, pointing to the cats curled up on chairs. "This was a rampage."

After dinner I drove to Marge's. Rapping on the screen door until my knuckles hurt, I yelled, "Are you there, Marge?" Maybe she really was sick.

She finally came to the door, tying the sash of a pink housecoat. "Carol, come in."

"After this afternoon, I got to worrying, and just wanted to make sure you were all right."

"Oh, don't worry about me, it's just the shock of the past two days telling on an old lady."

"Can we talk for a minute?" I asked.

"Certainly." She pushed open the aluminum screen door.

Bailey Boo, basking in the warmth of a crackling fire, raised his head and sniffed, cataloging my scent in a special file that only dogs have. "It's just me, Bailey Boo," I said softly from the foyer.

"I don't know what I'll do without him, when he goes. He's twelve now, he can't have many years left."

"My first pony lived to be thirty-two," I said. "I still miss him."

"After you called, I remembered it was because of Bailey that I met Randy. Bailey went off one day, sniffing around like he does, and ended up over by the lake. He was just beginning to go blind, and probably couldn't figure out where he was. Randy found my address on Bailey's tag, and brought him home."

"That was nice of him."

"I was so grateful, I'd been in a panic from the moment I knew he'd gone missing. We visited a bit and I fixed Randy dinner. I felt I owed him at least that much."

"How long ago was that?"

"Oh, I expect it was a couple years ago, I don't rightly know, for sure. Care for some sherry? We could sip it by the fire."

"Sounds lovely. The perfect end to a less-than-perfect day." I gratefully sank into an easy chair.

"I'll get us some—be right back," she said.

I looked around the room, at the gilt-framed fox hunting prints on the wall. Elegant and refined, just like Marge. She seemed such an unlikely match to befriend Randy, I thought, as she stepped into the room, carrying two crystal snifters. I let the amber wine slip down my throat slowly, savoring its sweetness. I asked, "So you became friends? You and Randy?"

"I felt sorry for him. He really was a kind, sweet man. The alcoholic was a shadow over the real person." She hesitated, and raised her glass to her lips. "It must have been awful, having an addiction hanging over his head, something he thought he couldn't live without. He was so sick, it was killing him slowly, torturing him."

Was she trying to tell me it was a blessing in disguise, putting an "it was for the best" spin on his death? Could the Marge I knew, who perhaps I didn't know as well as I thought, justify poisoning him in what she felt was an act of mercy?

She continued, "Life really is so sad, you know, even more so, nearer the end. You begin to wonder what your purpose is, what God has in store for you. Take me for example, what purpose do I serve?"

I'd never known Marge to be so morose. "Marge, do you really think you always know your own purpose in life? Maybe in subtle ways, ways you don't even realize,

you provide inspiration to people you never imagined."
People like me.

"Name one person who has benefited by my presence lately."

"Well, off the top of my head, Randy. You were kind to him when no one else cared."

"Look where it got him. Maybe when you get to be my age, you'll understand."

I steeled myself with a deep breath, mustering every ounce of tact and courage I could scrounge up, neither of which I've been overly endowed with according to Jack, and prayed I didn't hurt her. It was now or never. "Did you ever think he might have been better off dead?"

Her mouth quivered. For a moment I wasn't sure if she wanted to cry or spit nails. In the deafening silence, it seemed she teetered between the two, then pulled herself up rigidly, and in an icy tone said, "It's late and I think you'd better go."

"I'm sorry, I never meant to offend you."

She stood, and pointed to the door. "Now, Carol. Go!"

Choking back tears, I grabbed my purse and let myself out.

The sheriff called late Monday night, after I got back from Marge's, to tell me toxins had been recovered from the stomach contents, serum and urine of the deceased, showing the protoplasmic poison gyromitrin.

"Gyro-what?" I asked.

"Gyromitrin. *Gyromitra esculenta* or false morel, poisonous mushrooms that contain monomethylhydrazine, or MMH, a hydrazine derivative used in rocket fuel."

"Rocket fuel! Mushroom hunters flood these woods in late April and early May, searching for morels. Why on earth would they want them if they're poisonous?"

"There are morels and there are false morels. Two entirely different things. If you know what you're doing, you don't mix the two up. But the toxicologist tells me even a true morel can be deadly if it's grown in close proximity to a poisonous species. The MMH destroys the liver. Seems our fella ate them in spaghetti sauce Sunday night. Now my question is: If he was homeless, how'd he make spaghetti sauce? It's not exactly the type of thing you'd cook over a campfire."

Was he suggesting I'd poisoned him or was he on a fishing expedition? How was he to know Marge had already admitted to cooking Randy dinner when he returned Bailey? Had she made him dinner on a regular basis? *Most recently, Sunday night*? I knew what I had to do. "Marge Butler, my neighbor, knew him. She says his name was Randy, and his daughter lives in town. The sweater he was wearing belonged to Marge's late husband."

What's done is done, I told myself. I'd spilled my guts, and what he chose to do with the information was his business.

The sheriff gave a tired sigh. "I'll need you and your husband to stop by first thing in the morning, to make another statement, similar to the one on Sunday."

Great. There goes any friendship I ever had with Marge. "Sure. Can we come early, before work?"

"Six a.m., I'll be here." Another sigh.

"Any news on Julie's case?"

"Only what we already knew, cause of death was a gunshot wound, 357 Magnum. Entry point, the back, exited the chest. What's this Marge's phone number?"

I gave him her number and hung up. I said to Jack, "I don't know how much of that you heard or understood, but

Randy died from eating poisonous mushrooms in spaghetti sauce on Sunday night. Something about mushrooms used to produce rocket fuel. After what Marge told me tonight, I had to clue him in, but now I feel like a squealer."

"It was the right thing to do."

"That doesn't make me feel any less a traitor. I'm going to boot up the computer and see what I can find on false morels. I already forgot the toxic chemical name, something starting with a "G.""

My search proved fruitful a short time later, when I pulled up page after page of information on mushroom toxins. "Wow, Jack, come in here and read this." I called to him from the spare bedroom converted into a computer room. I read from the screen. "There are four categories of mushroom toxin: protoplasmic, neurotoxins, gastrointestinal irritants and disulfiram-like. False morels fall into the protoplasmic poisons, which are the most likely to be fatal or to cause irreversible organ damage. Certain species of false morel contain gyromitrin, a volatile hydrazine derivative. Symptoms usually manifest themselves eight to twelve hours after ingestion, with onset of abdominal pain, headache, vomiting and diarrhea."

"I knew there was a good reason why I never liked mushrooms," Jack said.

"And now I think I've got a good reason to join your dislike. But, listen, there's more: The toxin primarily attacks the liver, but there may be additional destruction of red blood cells and the central nervous system. Malfunction of the liver causes death in twenty to forty percent of the cases, usually in persons with reduced liver function due to alcoholism, age or other disability."

Jack stood behind me, reading over my shoulder. "There you have it. His drinking made him more susceptible to the poison."

"And look at this," I said, clicking farther down on the screen. "The early false morel is easily confused with the true morel."

"But what's this got to do with rocket fuel?"

"The sheriff said the toxin was a component of rocket fuel, something called monomethyl something, MMH, I think it was." I scrolled down, trying to find it.

Jack's eyes moved faster than my hand on the clicker, and he pointed to the screen. "Right there, monomethylhydrazine, a chemical found in rocket fuel. Its presence may occur in different quantities in different geographic regions and its affect may vary between individuals."

I looked up at Jack, and said, "Are you thinking what I'm thinking?"

"If Marge made poisonous spaghetti sauce, it must have been by accident."

"Except tonight, something told me she felt she was doing him a favor."

"Causing someone's liver to fail is doing them a favor?"

"If it was an accident, why didn't she get sick, too? Maybe she didn't eat the spaghetti because she knew there was a good reason not to eat it. If it was an accident, why wouldn't she admit it, instead of throwing me out of the house?"

"Maybe she's scared."

"I'd be scared, too, if I was her. She's got some explaining to do." I sent the pages to print, then shut down the computer and went to bed.

CHAPTER SEVEN

Tuesday sparkled under a cloudless cerulean sky. But in the instant of recollection that comes after waking, I remembered alienating a good friend. I wanted to shrink back into bed, pull the covers over me and hope the world would miraculously fix itself. No such luck. Julie and Randy were still dead, Jack was still upset about my riding alone, and Tuesday being Tuesday, there were animals that needed feeding and a job that needed doing. *And another statement to sign at the police station.* I groaned. By light of day, setting the sheriff on Marge's trail seemed absurd, but I couldn't shake the feeling she was somehow involved in Randy's death.

While the horses dove into pails of oats, I lingered in the doorway of the stable, watching three killdeer chicks. Fluffy cotton balls on toothpick legs, they scurried in circles, their mother limping and fluttering and doing her best to divert my attention. Dew drops danced along blades of green grass and fell dripping, swallowed up whole into the earth again.

Chet was at his closing, so I spent the day cleaning up a pile of half-finished jobs thrown aside on Monday. Counting the minutes to four o'clock, I raced home to change into riding jeans, hoping that if I gave Feather a quick grooming, I'd have enough time before dark to look for Julie's tape recorder.

Popping a roast with hastily quartered carrots and potatoes into the oven, I set the temperature on low. I'd deal with Jack when I got back, figuring the riding issue would go one of two ways. Either he'd take the silent route and skirt the entire issue, or there would be another argument. My bet was he would take the easy route; he'd stay quiet.

I yanked on boot pulls, struggling with riding boots that were no longer the same size and shape as the legs they'd been custom made to fit twenty years ago. The cats lounged on the deck, basking in the warm sun. Hannibal dropped a decapitated mouse next to my foot. "My God, Hannibal, why must you eat only the heads?"

Feather was in the back pasture, her head down in the grass, casually flicking her tail from side to side. She daintily took the carrot I offered. "Might as well enjoy your time out here, before bug season starts," I told her, slipping the halter over her head. "Two months from now, you and Echo will be stomping at flies and trying to stay cool."

Dust clouds rose, while I curried and brushed her, then curried and brushed again. By the time I made a final swipe over her with a damp cloth, wisps of hair and dust formed an outline of her body on the asphalt stable floor, like the chalk outline at a crime scene. I lifted the heavy German saddle from its rack and onto her back.

Past Marge's was an overgrown field where an old farmhouse had burned, leaving only the charred foundation. A poplar tree, somehow unscathed by the fire, fluttered its silvery leaves, like wind chimes, in the breeze. I turned into the driveway, then through the field and cut over to the trail into the forest.

A thick woody vine coiled around a dogwood tree and hung suspended from the top branch. The path under the vine sloped downhill, into a damp valley spotted with Trilliums. A purple Jack-in-the-Pulpit stood at the edge of the path, one tiny wooden soldier guarding its three-leafed stalk in a sea of ivory. We climbed a steep hill, almost out of the valley, but still in the cool shadows.

A stone wall lay ahead, a reminder of when this land was farmed and the fields divided. Abruptly, Feather stopped, throwing her head up, ears forward. I stiffened, expecting her to shy or bolt. Standing on the wall, a man reached into the branches of a massive oak tree, bracing one knee against the oak's rough trunk.

I held Feather back, waiting. One corner of a black trash bag was secured underneath his belt. He pulled something from the tree, looked at it, and dropped it into the open corner of the plastic bag, shaking the bag to settle the object to the bottom.

Feather snorted when he shook the bag and it drew his attention. Though I hadn't seen him in years, I knew him. He looked a lot like Kathy, his hair was the same shade of blond and he'd grown incredibly tall and thin.

I rode Feather into the light, out of the valley. "Derrick?" I asked. "Remember me? I'm Carol Ward, your mom's friend."

Jumping down, he said, "Yeah, I remember." His jeans hung loosely from a gaunt waist. "Nice horse; what's its name?"

"*It* is a mare, and her name is Feather."

He pulled the corner of the plastic bag out from under his belt. Feather stood her ground but eyed him warily.

"Does she spook easily?" he asked.

"She's usually fairly calm."

"You just never know about them, do you?" He took a step toward us and Feather took a step backward. The bag rustled as he walked.

"No, I guess you don't," I said, wondering where this was leading.

"You're not afraid, in the woods, all by yourself?"

"I don't scare easily."

"I guess you'd be in a real pickle if you got thrown, and maybe hurt, way out here, not a soul around. A person could lay here all night, maybe longer."

"My husband knows exactly where I am," I lied. "And if I don't show up at a certain time, he knows exactly where to look for me." If you're going to lie, might as well go all the way, I told myself. "Besides, he insists I carry a cell phone." *Which would work out nicely if you didn't forget it ninety-nine percent of the time.*

"I can see the headlines now," he said. Spreading his arms wide, as if reading from a billboard, he said, "Second Body Found in Remote State Park." He laughed.

"My, aren't you morbid," I said. His choice of conversation *did* have me alarmed, but damn if I was going to show it. "I said I don't scare easily."

"Tell the truth. I think you're just as afraid as she was."

"Who?" I asked.

"Julie, of course."

"How would you know?" Discreetly, I gripped a handful of Feather's mane. If she bolted, I wanted to make sure I went with her.

"That's just it, isn't it? I don't know. It's all speculation. The world is full of it. Nobody knows anything about anything. We're all just little rats, running a maze."

"That's a rather pessimistic outlook on life."

He shrugged his shoulders. "Just calling it like I see it."

I shifted the conversation. "What brings you out here? I don't often see people on foot this far back."

He rubbed a gouge in the soft dirt with the toe of his hiking boot. His eyes were downcast. "I went for a walk yesterday and lost my dad's Swiss Army knife. I was hoping I'd find it."

"Are those the red knives with the white cross?"

"Yeah. Some have all sorts of tools, and silverware and scissors, but this one was pretty basic, just a couple of real sharp blades."

Just what I wanted to see returned to his hands—a couple of real sharp blades. "If I find it, I'll let you know." I steeled myself and pressed shaky knees against Feather's sides. "I've got to get back before dark. You should do the same. Say hello to your mom, will you?"

"Sure."

Feather left as wide a berth as possible around him. I prayed he didn't see my trembling fingers.

"Carol?" It seemed an intrusion that he called me by name.

I turned. "Yeah?"

"Now that I'm staying with my mom, I'm hoping to start riding her gelding. He hasn't been worked in months."

The Derrick I remembered couldn't have cared less about his mom's horse, or riding.

"Maybe we can ride together sometime?" he asked. "Just you and me?"

"Yeah, sure. Give me a call. Your mom has my number." I wondered if he'd ever call. But even more, I wondered why he'd been out walking yesterday, when it rained all day, and why he was lying about the knife. And most of all, I wondered what was in the trash bag.

I rode into the Tamaracks, looking behind me at first, checking to see if he followed me. Circling the outside perimeter of yellow tape pulled between the trees, I checked the places I'd put a tape recorder, if I'd been recording songbirds—in the trees, on a rock or a stump, on the ground, beside a fallen log. Wherever it was, I hoped it wasn't ruined in yesterday's downpour.

The sun melted low on the horizon, and with the rose-blue dusk, came a chill I couldn't shake, reminding me it was time to turn back.

Kathy's car was parked in Rene's drive, next to one with a rental plate. I rode in as they came out the front door. Short and plump, Rene had a round, cherub face and ruddy complexion.

"Hello, Carol," Rene called.

Kathy waived. She tossed an overnight bag into the back of her car. Rolling down the driver side window, she said, "Rene, be sure to call if you need anything."

"I should be fine, now that Ron's here. Go home and get some rest. You've been here three days and I know you've got problems of your own."

"I just saw Derrick in the woods," I said to Kathy.

"Whereabouts?" she asked.

"By that huge old oak tree, next to the stone wall. He said he was searching for a lost knife."

Rene looked at Kathy and Kathy looked at me. Unspoken questions seemed to jump between us.

"That kid would lose his head if it weren't attached," Kathy laughed nervously. "I'd better get home." She headed down the gravel drive, her red tail lights flickering in-between the boughs of pines lining the drive.

"That goes for me, too, about calling if you need anything or if I can help in any way," I said.

"Actually, Carol, there is one thing." Rene fiddled with the zipper pull on her nylon jacket. "I ordered a birthstone ring for Julie's birthday next month. We'd been to the jeweler in town and she chose the one she wanted, but it had to be sized. They called last week to say it was ready, I just never made it into town to pick it up." Her lip trembled. "The funeral service is on Friday and I'd like her to be buried wearing it. I can't face going in there. It's silly, I know, but I just can't do it." She hesitated for a moment, then her voice cracked, "I picture myself standing there, looking over the counter, and suddenly she's there, beside me, like before."

I wanted to end her agony. "I'll get it," I said. "Do I need some sort of claim ticket?"

She nodded. "Hang on; it's in the house. While you're here, I'd like to introduce you to Julie's father, too."

By a faint trace of acrid smoke, I knew someone in the neighborhood burned a wood fire and somehow, in the mixture of the evening chill, the smell of the wood fire and the cry of the owl in Lyle's barn, the night seemed hauntingly beautiful, yet lonely and sad and foreboding, like the end of a day late in fall, when winter hangs in the shadows.

The storm door slammed. "Carol, this is Ron," Rene said. In his late forties, his weathered face was handsome in a rugged sort of way. The blue jeans and pearl snap shirt he wore needed only a cowboy hat and chaps and he could have been the Marlboro man.

I awkwardly stuck out my hand. "Hello," I said.

"Pleased to meet you," he said.

He sounded like what I thought the Marlboro man would sound like, too, a Waylon Jennings voice, low and calm. One of Feather's ears flicked forward when his big hand brushed her neck.

"Mighty fine animal you've got here; no doubt about that."

I smiled and found myself liking him, and I could tell Feather liked him too, mostly because her ears weren't flat back like they were when Echo gets too close.

Rene handed me the claim tag. "I really appreciate this, Carol."

Ron asked, "What's that?"

Her sad eyes crinkled in the corners when she smiled. "Carol's going to run an errand for me."

Lifting the ticket, I said, "I'll bring it over on Thursday, after work."

I twisted around in the saddle to wave good-bye. They looked easy standing side by side, like they belonged with one another.

CHAPTER EIGHT

"I'm taking you out for dinner."

"Huh? On a weeknight? We never go out on weeknights." I pulled off my riding boots and added them to the line-up in the mud room. "What about the pot roast?"

"It had an accident."

"Jack, how does a pot roast have an accident?" If he thought I didn't recognize the smell of burnt beef, he was wrong. Nonetheless, I decided to go along. Sometimes his explanations were entertaining.

"I thought it was cooking too slow, so I turned the oven up just a little and then went down to the basement to sand and stain my new book case."

No further explanation necessary. The man practically needed a heat shield to re-enter the universe after a trip to his basement carpenter shop, that's how completely absorbed he became with his projects. Dr. Franken Ward, as I teasingly called him, frequently lost track of time in his quasi-laboratory. "How long were you down there?"

"It couldn't have been more than a few minutes."

Hours was probably more accurate.

"It wasn't long at all, and when I came back upstairs, the meat was, well, it was slightly overcooked."

"Slightly overcooked? As in not edible?"

"You might say so. But I'll let you decide for yourself." He lifted the lid of the blue speckled roasting pan. A charred lump lay atop a bed of shriveled black carrots and rock-hard potatoes.

"For crying out loud, Jack, it looks like it caught fire!"

"Almost, but not quite."

I grabbed my purse. "Let's go, I'm hungry!"

I slowed the little pickup to a crawl. Picketers, milling on the sidewalk in front of the Town Hall, carrying signs, leaning against signs, wearing sandwich board signs, chanting and marching, formed a loop from the feed store, to the Post Office, then back to the Town Hall.

"What the heck is going on in town?" Jack asked.

"Looks like some kind of protest."

"Protesting what? Higher feed prices?" Jack asked.

I squinted, reading one of the sandwich boards. "This didn't… need… this didn't need to happen. What's that supposed to mean?" I asked Jack.

"You got me."

"Look," I pointed out the window, "There's Dr. Adler. What does his sign say?"

"Something about birth control."

"Birth control? What on earth?" I pulled over to the curb for a closer look. "You'd better get your eyes checked. It doesn't say birth control, it says gun control, Gun Control Now." I parked and we approached Dr. Adler, who, typically theatrical, marched unnecessarily high like a stringhalted horse or an overly zealous drum major, pulsing his sign up and down with each step. "What's going on?"

"Gun control. We need gun control now!" he chanted.

A woman picketer went around Dr. Adler, who, by stopping to talk, was backing up the loop. Her sign read, "Too late for Julie—Who's Next?"

"This poor girl's death was unnecessary. If nobody had a gun we'd all be safer, we'd all sleep easier at night! Too many guns!" he yelled, even though I was less than a foot away.

I saw Jack's hackles raising, like a bobcat backed against a hen house wall and staring down the business end of a farmer's pitchfork. "You're crazy! You're all crazy!" Jack said. "Taking guns away from honest citizens, because of too many murders, is like closing all the fast food restaurants because too many people are fat. Taking away choices doesn't force people to do the right thing. The crooks will still be able to get guns illegally, it's the good, honest citizens like you and me who'll be hurt, with no way to defend ourselves."

The loop was really backed up now. An angry, loud mob milled around Jack. "Let it go!" I pleaded with him. "C'mon, I'm hungry. Let's go." I left him and got into the truck, hoping he'd follow.

"Dipshits! This town's filled with freakin' idiots wanting to micromanage the world. None of 'em got a lick of sense." Jack slammed his door. "What's this country coming to, anyway?"

"Don't get so excited. Nobody's taking anything away yet. They have the right of free speech, too, just like you."

"But if today they take away our handguns and our hunting rifles, what do they take away tomorrow?"

He had a point. "We'll cross that bridge when we get to it, and fortunately, we're not there yet." I pulled into the only sit-down, served-by-a-waitress restaurant our town had, and waved to the sheriff, in a corner booth by the window. A week ago, I barely knew the man existed, now I saw him every day. I said to Jack, "I wonder if he knows about the protest."

"Be kind of hard to miss, in a town this size."

"I'll have the roasted pepper pita pocket and a cup of decaf," I told the bubble-gum snapping waitress who appeared at our table.

After Jack ordered, I said, "I'm going to see if the sheriff found Randy's daughter and if there's going to be a funeral service."

"For crying out loud, let the man eat his dinner in peace. The way it's been going around here lately, that's getting harder and harder to do. People dying and being murdered and now those knotheads snarling up traffic on Main Street."

"He's a public servant. They don't get any peace." I slid into the booth across from the sheriff.

"Howdy, Miss Carol."

"Evening, sheriff." His tuna sandwich combo mesmerized me. "I don't want to disturb your dinner or anything, but I was wondering if you found Randy's daughter."

"Sure did. I asked Miss Dodds, over at the Post Office, if she knew an older fella named Randy, who lived with his daughter in town, and she spit the name and address right out, just like a computer."

"How'd she take it? The daughter, I mean."

He munched a potato chip. "About like you'd expect. Real upset, sad, but didn't come as a shock. She knew better'n anybody the kind of life he led. She's having a memorial mass Friday morning at St. Anne's. Remains have been cremated."

"Julie's service is on Friday, too. Wouldn't you know, I don't go to a funeral in years, then suddenly there's two in one day. When it rains, it pours."

He snapped another potato chip. No wonder he was paunchy, at approximately one gram of fat per chip. I watched his jaws grind sideways, like a horse that needs its teeth floated.

"Still a puzzle, though, who cooked that spaghetti sauce. Been weighing on me heavy, that, and the girl's death, too," he said.

CHAPTER NINE

There was no time to ride on Wednesday. The blacksmith was due at the barn at five o'clock, and although Matt was never on time, if by some odd chance he showed up and I wasn't there, I'd be another three months rescheduling. Six-thirty came and went without him, while Feather and Echo waited, munching hay in their stalls.

An hour later his truck bumped up and over my lawn, and, sliding to a stop, left a six-foot skid mark on the grass. I screamed, certain my barn was about to be mowed down. The horses cringed in the far corners of their stalls. A pop can tumbled out when he opened the door, and someone had scrawled "test dirt" in the grime over the wheel well.

"Sorry I'm late." Unruly black curls popped out from under a smudged baseball cap advertising "Co-Op Feed & Seed." "Would you mind if I shoe one horse and come back on Saturday for the other one? My back is aching."

I opened my mouth to answer, but wasn't fast enough.

"Which one do you want done today? You're my last stop and my wrist is killing me."

I thought it was his back. "Geez, Matt, for a man in your thirties, you certainly have a multitude of medical problems. Do Feather, her shoes are shot."

He pulled tight around his stubby legs the strings of his leather farrier's apron, and lowering the tailgate of his truck, slid an anvil out. "Did you hear about the murder on the bridle paths?" he asked.

"Hear about it? My riding partner, Denise, and I found her."

"The body? You found the body?" He stared at me, spellbound, like a deer caught in headlights. "What was it like?" he asked.

Why are some people only interested in blood and guts? "I'd rather not discuss the details, if you don't mind."

"I've been following it, and today the newspaper said she was recording song birds and the police can't find the tape recorder."

My mouth dropped open. "How'd they find out about it?"

"How'd who find out about what?" he asked.

"The newspapers. How'd they find out about the tape recorder?"

"Beats me. What's the big deal, whether anybody knows or not?" He slammed his tailgate shut and a hunk of rust fell to the ground.

I followed him into the barn. "The big deal is, it bought the police some time, in finding a tape that might have recorded the killer's voice. Now every do-gooder from here to Timbuktu is going to be looking for it, trying to get his name in the newspaper."

He hooked Feather's hoof between his knees, scraping away mud with a stiff brush. "Is Jack home?" he asked.

Feather sniffed my pocket for carrots. "Yeah, why?"

"His name came up on a list of local NRA members. I'm the regional chairman, and we're organizing a rally to protest these anti-gun perverts prancing around town."

"Don't get him started. We went to dinner last night and he almost ended up in a fight outside Town Hall."

"Those people are real jerks."

"I'll tell you the same thing I told Jack, and I'm not taking sides, I'm just stating a fact—they have the same right to a peaceful protest that you and your gun club have, *peaceful* being the operative word."

"And that's what we're doing—exercising our right to assemble in public."

"Are you sure your members aren't too hot-headed for this?" Red-neck came to mind, and as much as I hated the term, no other description seemed appropriate.

"Not to worry. It's all worked out, down to a schedule and everything, which is why I need to talk to Jack." Putting Feather's hoof down, he straightened up, then stretched backward, and pulled a creased paper from his wallet. Unfolding it, he asked, "What hours can he picket tomorrow? We're doing two-hour shifts, from noon to ten p.m."

"He doesn't get home from work until five-thirty."

"Good, I'll put him down for six to eight." His grimy fingers pulled a pen from his shirt pocket.

"You'd better talk to him first," I said.

"Yeah, sure. Say, Carol, do you still have the old shoes we took off her last fall? Maybe we can use them over, so I won't have to make new ones."

"Matt, for crying out loud, I'm paying you for new shoes!"

He held up a stretch-bandaged arm. "I don't think my wrist·can take pounding out a new pair today. How about I cut ten dollars off the bill?"

"I don't want a bargain, I want the horse shod!"

"And that's what you're getting. Just old shoes instead of new. Small difference."

I threw my hands up. Forty minutes later Matt clinched the last nail on Feather. He loaded his equipment, conveniently leaving the pop can on my lawn. Pulling a dog-eared spiral calendar from under the visor, he said, "You can pay me when I come back to shoe the gelding. How's Saturday, about two-thirty?"

Thinking he may have just made a tactical error, I quickly said, "Two-thirty's fine." Delaying payment would ensure he'd show up instead of calling with some flimsy, last-minute excuse.

"Where's Jack?"

"He's around somewhere; probably glued to the television. Don't drive over the septic tank on your way out," I reminded him.

He waved, gunned the big dually and drove out, directly over the septic tank.

My hand was on the nearest rock within seconds. I hurled it at his receding truck, but it fell sadly short of its target and I succeeded only in wrenching my arm from the socket. "Do I speak Upper Swahili, Matt?" I screamed. Damn that man!

Rubbing my sore shoulder, I filled grain buckets for morning feeding, packed the hay rack and let the horses out.

It was a warm evening. Max played in the daffodil bed, pressing the stems down, then swatted at the mangled flowers as they bounced back. Jack lounged on the deck, his feet up on the railing, and through the screened patio door George Jones belted out something about a good year for roses. The grill sizzled.

"Sure smells good, whatever it is," I said.

"Chicken. Done in the barn?"

"Yes, thank God. Feather's shod and he's coming back Saturday for Echo."

Jack crushed his beer can, aimed and made a basket into the recycling bin. "He drove over the septic tank again. Didn't you tell him not to?"

"If I've told him once, I've told him a million times. Maybe I need to write a note and pin it to his forehead."

"I gave him the message myself this time, and if he does it again, I'll be pinning something to his forehead, and it's not going to be a note. What's his problem, is he learning disabled?"

"He should be so lucky as to have an excuse. It's scary to think he's the chairman of your gun club. They actually let someone that dumb carry a weapon?"

"Your green eyes are beautiful when you're all fired up."

I pretended to ignore his flattery.

He abruptly changed the subject. "I'm not happy about your choice to continue riding alone in the woods, but I guess I can't stop you."

So it wasn't to be forgotten. I gave him a big bear hug. "Thanks for understanding." I sat down to pull off my boots. "Are you walking in the rally?"

"Six to eight p.m."

"Don't get yourself into hot water. It's a simple, peaceful rally; you carry your sign and they carry theirs. No yelling—no hitting."

He kissed my forehead. "Peaceful, I promise. You won't have to bail me out of jail."

"I'd better not. Our savings account is down to zip."

"So what's new?" he asked.

"If you get thrown in the clink, you're on your own."

"Spoken like a true, loving wife."

I shrugged. "Just being realistic." The screen door flew off the track when I slid it open. Jack picked it up and popped it back in, following me into the house.

"Matt said today's newspaper reported the police still haven't found the tape recorder. Who do you think spilled the beans?" I asked.

"Don't look at me," he said, raising two fingers in scout's honor.

The potato pot, boiling on the stove, hissed and spit and overflowed. I flicked the burner off and Jack grabbed the pot, holding it over the sink until the foamy water settled.

"I'll call Denise later. She's my pipeline to Kathy, and Kathy's the pipeline to everybody else."

After dinner, I tried Denise's number, but the phone rang and rang. She can't be asleep, I thought, it's only nine-thirty. Finally, she answered. "You weren't in bed already, were you?" I asked.

"Don't I wish. We just finished putting the new stall mats in." She sounded as tired as I felt. "They must weigh two hundred pounds each."

"Installing them is a pain, but they'll make a big difference in the amount of bedding used and the time it takes to muck out. And no more quagmires in the center of the stalls."

"That'll be a blessing."

"You probably haven't had dinner yet, so I'll get to the point—the stuff about the tape recorder leaked. Matt says it was in today's paper and if that motor mouth knows, so does everyone within a three-county radius."

"I didn't tell a soul," she said.

"Me neither," I said.

"Todd's in the clear, too; the only place he's been is the hospital."

"How's his mom?" I asked.

"They're starting some new treatment and warned us the first two weeks would be brutal, so between Todd and his sisters, somebody's staying with her all the time. She's holding her own right now.

Getting back to the tape recorder, though, I don't know who could have told—there were so few of us that knew. You and I should go out there and look for it."

"I went yesterday, but I didn't have much time. I *did* find a Jack-in-the-Pulpit, though. And an ocean of trilliums."

Avid wildflower lovers, we both carried field guides in the pockets of our saddle pads. "Trilliums are my favorite," she said, "It's too bad they only bloom such a short time. I hope I see them before they're faded."

"Want to ride after work tomorrow?" I asked.

"Love to, but I'm hauling my sister's horse to Davison for her riding lesson, to some guy who's supposed to be fantastic with western pleasure horses, I forget his name. I promised her two weeks ago I'd take her, so I can hardly back out now."

"Maybe we'll ride Saturday or Sunday," I said.

"Jack-in-the-Pulpit is a very rare flower. I should probably tell Kathy, so she can tag it as an endangered species. Where was it?"

"In the deep, wet valley, before the stone wall. Something was really strange, though—Derrick was standing on the stone wall."

"What's so strange about that?" she asked.

"He said he lost his knife. Just seemed odd he'd lose it there."

"He's probably bored and went for a long walk. Kathy says he's enrolled in summer semester at the community college, but classes don't start for another month."

"It wasn't just the fact he was there."

"What then?"

"The conversation was really bizarre, like he was amusing himself by frightening me. And I'm sure he lied about the knife."

"Why would he lie?"

"I know you've always thought I had something against him, but this was more than that—it was totally different and I didn't imagine it. He dropped something into a garbage bag and then he shook the bag and asked if Feather spooked easily, while he walked toward us, rustling the bag. I believe he was trying to get me thrown."

"What on earth for?"

"How do I know? Then he said I was probably just as scared as Julie. It was a weird conversation."

"Does sound a bit odd."

"Maybe Derrick knows something we don't?" I speculated.

"I wonder if he opens up to Kathy. I know they haven't had the best of relationships in the past.

Oh, Carol, I almost forgot to tell you—lock up everything around your place. We got broken into yesterday, middle of the day."

"No kidding! What'd they take?"

"The new wide-screen television we got for Christmas and Todd's good watch. I went through my jewelry box and didn't notice anything gone, but the only jewelry I've ever had worth anything is my wedding ring, and I never take that off."

"What's going on?" I asked. "This neighborhood's getting downright dangerous."

"Sheriff Morton said it's the seventh robbery in the last two months, all within a ten-mile radius and always the same things stolen—jewelry and electronics, and guns, if they're around."

"We're safe as far as jewelry and electronics, unless someone other than the Smithsonian wants an ancient twenty-three inch television, a rinky-dink CD player and a turntable record-player. Guns are a different story. Jack seems to be accumulating more and more of them."

"Who can figure? They took a seven-hundred-dollar television but left a twelve-hundred-dollar show saddle."

"They're looking for things that are easy to fence. Not much market for show saddles. Where were those two monster-size dogs of yours?" I watched Jack spray lubricant on the track of the patio door, then work the door back and forth.

"Wouldn't you know, it was the one day we put them in the kennel. Most of the time we leave them in the house, if we're not gone too long."

"Sounds like it's somebody who hangs around, watching when people come and go." The screen door flew off the track again.

"Now that's a lovely thought—that someone's watching our every move. Though, at this point, I guess we're safe—they've already taken what they want from us. Still, it gives you a creepy feeling to know somebody's been in your house and rummaged through your stuff," she said.

"Before I forget to ask you, "When is Julie's memorial service?"

"It's on Friday, I know that. Hang on a second," she said. "Kathy stuck a note in my door yesterday. I think it gave the time. It's here somewhere. Here it is—it starts at eleven."

"You going?" I asked.

"Sure. I took the day off. What's Jack yelling about?" she asked.

"The sliding glass door. Lots of excitement around here lately. Do you remember the old guy we've seen picking pop cans over by the lake?" I didn't wait for her answer, but rushed on, "Early Monday morning, I found him, unconscious, in our hay loft. We figure he must have been trying to get in out of the rain. We called 911 and they took him to the hospital, but he died a couple hours later. Coroner says he was poisoned."

"Poisoned! Who would do that?"

"That's what we'd like to know. But I'll tell you one thing, there's something strange about Marge lately. I found out, in a roundabout way, that she's been making him dinner on Sunday nights, but when I asked her a couple questions, she threw me out of the house."

"Threw you out of the house? Marge? What'd you do, ask her if *she* poisoned him?"

"Not in those exact words, but sort of." Suddenly the ticking of the kitchen clock seemed unusually loud. The other end of the line had gone dead. "Denise? Hello? Are you there?" I asked.

"Will you ever learn? Why don't you buy an industrial-size roll of duct tape and put a piece over your mouth, first thing, every morning?"

"I know, I know," I said. "Don't make me feel worse than I already do."

Todd said something to Denise in the background. "Carol, I've got to go. Todd says Kathy's at the door, she's crying and really upset. I guess the police have taken Derrick in for questioning."

"That's awful. Call me at work tomorrow."

"Yeah, sure, first chance I get."

CHAPTER TEN

Remnants of morning haze hung low in valleys of green. Listening to the muffled whinnies of Rene's horses, mine nickered in answer. The temperature was supposed to hit seventy today, and thinking ahead to the afternoon reminded me I'd promised to pick up Julie's ring. The bright sun had me so energized, that I got on the road early, stopped for a donut, and still had time to spare.

"Thank God you're here!" Howard, lead counsel for the real estate department, said, holding open the door to the lobby.

Right then and there, I should've turned around, gotten back into my truck and gone home. If I'd been smart, that is. "That sounds fairly ominous," I said. I set my waxed bakery sack on the counter, hitched the strap of my purse up my shoulder, and signed in at the front desk. "Whatever it is, my donut comes first," I said. It was still ten minutes to eight and normally I wouldn't even be here yet.

"I'll make a fresh pot of coffee while you find out what's wrong with the computers," Howard said.

"*Please* tell me you haven't been doing your own word processing again." I waited. "Howard?"

"I was only trying to help. The Maxwell closing's at one, and I just found out it's really not Maxwell at all, it's

Maxell, and I thought I'd give you and Lora a jump on revising the documents by fixing the misspelled names, and—"

"Their name isn't Maxwell?" I asked in disbelief. "It's your client, Howard, how could you not know what their name is? And just what *is* wrong with the computers?"

"Like I said, I was trying to search and replace the name, you know, change Maxwell to Maxell, and something happened. Anyway, I think we've lost the Purchase Agreement. I'm going to make that coffee right now." He whisked down the hall, toward the kitchen.

I was in hot pursuit. "Lost the Purchase Agreement? The *fifty-five page* Purchase Agreement? Lost, as in *deleted*?"

"I'm not sure lost is the correct word. The computer said something about a fatal error."

"My God, Howard, the closing is in five hours!"

Lora and I typed furiously through our lunch hours to meet the deadline, but by then I had a splitting headache. At one o'clock Howard waited for the elevator to the third-floor conference room, briefcase in hand, and smiling, gave us a thumbs-up. "Dipshit!" Lora muttered under her breath. "He had weeks to finalize those papers, but instead waited until the morning of the closing to announce the buyer's name is spelled wrong!" We walked through the lobby and back to our cubicles.

The receptionist buzzed me. "Carol, you've got a call. It's Denise."

Perfect timing, I thought. Although I'd been expecting to hear from her all morning, I wouldn't have had time to talk to her anyway, so it worked out better that she called now. "Hi, Denise, what's the news?"

"The police took Derrick in for questioning. They found the print of a hiking boot matching Derrick's, near the body."

"That's all they've got to go on?"

"No, there's more. Julie's autopsy report gave the time of death between one and two on Saturday afternoon."

I tried to remember where I was between one and two on Saturday. "Denise, remember, you had to be home by two because you were going to the hospital to see Todd's mom? We took the trail through the pine forest sometime between one and two on Saturday, and that's where Julie's body was found! But how can that be? We didn't see anyone, and I never heard any gunshots, did you?"

"No, I can't say I did."

I tried to organize my thoughts, but my brain refused any attempts at coherence. "How could we have been so close and not seen or heard anything?"

"We were talking," Denise said, "And cantering, and you know how the wind whistles when you canter. Maybe we missed the gunshot. Or maybe they've got the time screwed up. Pathologists can make mistakes too, can't they? But because Kathy was at work Saturday afternoon, she can't say for sure where Derrick was, to give him an alibi."

"Where does he say he was?" I asked.

"He says was trying to hunt down a buddy of his he hadn't seen since before moving to Detroit. The friend's parents relocated and he talked with several of their old neighbors, trying to get their new address. He doesn't even know the neighbors by name, he just went door to door, asking."

"How is Kathy handling all of this?" I asked.

"She's really upset, and understandably so. It isn't fair. Derrick is never going to straighten out if everyone always expects the worst from him."

"Truthfully though, Denise, I can't say I trust him. And he was acting awfully strange in the woods the other day."

"Stealing is one thing, and I admit he's had a problem with that in the past, but now we're talking murder!"

"What motive could he have for killing Julie? Did he even know her?"

"He'd seen her out riding and asked Kathy who she was. Kathy says Derrick called Julie last Friday and wanted to take her to the movies, but Julie said no. He seemed a little peeved and left the house in a bad mood. They can't possibly think he'd shoot her for not wanting to date him!"

"You're right, that's just plain ridiculous," I said.

"That's not all—there was another break-in over on Hegel Road Friday night, and they're trying to pin that on him, too."

"Didn't the robberies start in February?" I asked. "Derrick only just got back in town last week, so how could he have been involved in those?"

"I'm telling you, the kid can't win."

"Where does he say he went Friday night?" This was getting confusing.

"He says he went to the movie alone."

"So, basically, what we're looking at here, is he's a suspect in both a murder and a robbery because he has no one to vouch for his whereabouts on either Friday night or Saturday afternoon." That sounded like guilty until proven innocent, contrary to the basis of our criminal justice system. I was thinking Derrick needed an attorney, and soon. "Have they arrested him?" I asked.

"No, the police are just questioning him for now."

"Has Kathy contacted an attorney?"

"I don't think so."

"We're a corporate law firm, but Chet can probably get a referral for Derrick."

I heard a horse's shrill whinny in the background. Denise worked greenies and hot walked for a reining horse trainer. "I gotta' go," she said. "This horse needs cooling out. I'll tell Kathy you're getting the name of a lawyer and I'll call you tonight if I hear anything more."

Leaving work at four sharp, I hurried to the parking lot. I had a full schedule ahead: get Julie's ring and deliver it to Rene, pass Chet's referral on to Kathy, buy carrots, and have Echo exercised before dark. And, although Marge and I hadn't spoken since Monday, I always picked up her grocery shopping list and coupons on Thursdays, so at some point, as much as I dreaded it, I was going to have to call her.

I pulled into town, parking across from the jewelry store. Anti-gun protesters marched single file on the sidewalk in front of the post office and now the pro-gun faction rallied across the street. I counted eight anti-gun protesters and five pro-gun. Jack's tour of duty was supposed to start at six—an hour from now. Calmness seemed to prevail, but I wondered how long that would last. It was a potentially volatile situation, with the two groups across the street from each other.

The sign in the jeweler's window said he closed at five-thirty, so I hurried inside. A string of bells hanging from the door jingled and slapped against the glass. Cigarette smoke permeated the air, explaining the grimy yellow film on the windows. Strangely, no one seemed to be minding the store, though I doubted jewelry would be left unattended for long.

I dug into my purse for the claim tag. The room was arranged in a three-sided configuration, two long glass cases on both sides, and a shorter one across the front, with an opening to a hallway. A man's voice emanated from the back and I stepped between a narrow break in the side and front showcase, peering around the corner. At the end of the hall a telephone cord stretched across an open doorway. Loud enough for me to hear at the opposite end of the hall, he said, "It's too soon; don't do anything yet."

What was too soon? Was he holding off on a diamond deal, waiting for prices to drop? Afraid my snooping might be discovered, I hurried back to the salesroom, catching my heel on a vacuum cleaner cord that had been left plugged into the wall. On the counter I spotted a metal bell, and jammed my thumb down hard on it, several times, until I heard footsteps in the hallway. How he stayed in business, when a customer could barely get him into the sales room, was a mystery to me.

His blond hair was raked into the oily rows left by a wide-toothed comb. Deeply tanned skin set off his expensive-looking gold watch and massive diamond dinner ring, yellow polo shirt and tan chinos. He looked more like a West Palm Beacher than the proprietor of a dingy jewelry store who did his own vacuuming.

"What can I do for you?" he asked, with a peculiar way of continually smiling, like something unbeknownst to me was humorous.

I slapped the claim tag down. "I'm here to pick this up."

He picked up the ticket. "Just a moment, I'll be right back." He stepped through the doorway to the back room, returning with a small manila envelope. "Was this the ring for the girl that was killed?" He laid the envelope on the counter.

I watched his eyes for some sign, some hint of sorrow or loss, and finding none, I said, "Murdered, she was murdered, while tape recording bird songs for a biology project."

His smile faded, like his tan, which now seemed a couple shades paler. "They've taken someone in for questioning," I said, sliding the ring from the envelope.

An emerald, May's birthstone, it was as green and vibrant and beautiful as the spring grass Julie would never again see. A birthday gift for a birthday she'd never have.

He clasped his hands in front of himself, and I saw where the flesh was white under the pressure of his fingers. "Someone's been arrested?" he asked. "I read the newspaper on Monday, but I don't remember anything about a tape recorder." His ice-blue eyes pierced me with an intensity that left me feeling violated.

"It wasn't supposed to be public knowledge, but the press got wind of it, and no, he hasn't been arrested, they're just questioning him, at this point." I turned the ring under the light, watching its refracted image throw rectangles of green on the glass countertop. "Personally, I think they've got the wrong man." I said.

"What makes you say that?"

Dropping the ring back into the envelope, I said, "Just a feeling I have."

"Have they found the tape recorder?" he asked. He put the ring into a dark velvet box.

"Nope. It's a big area to cover. It'll probably take awhile, unless somebody gets lucky."

He reached over the counter, took my hand in his, and said, "You know, I can fix that for you, so it won't turn on your finger."

My wedding ring, a marquis-shaped diamond, always turned a bit off center, so the stone brushed against my little finger. Embarrassed, I pulled my hand back. "It's been this way for fourteen years now, it's hardly worth fixing now. Was there a charge for the emerald?" I asked, remembering too late Rene telling me there wasn't.

"No charge," he said, smiling a smile that never reached his eyes, and my father's voice, from somewhere in the far reaches of my mind, reminded me, *Carol, never trust anyone whose smile doesn't make the skin around their eyes crinkle.*

"Thanks," I said, turning to leave, feeling his eyes bore holes through my back. I opened the door, but tripped on an untied shoelace, and letting the door close in front of me, I crouched down on one knee to tie it.

Then I heard his voice from the back, angry and loud. "I told you, it's too soon! I'm not taking any chances just because you're in a hurry for your money. You'll get paid when I get paid. Let the whole thing blow over, give the police some time to cool off."

My heart skipped a beat and I held my breath, afraid to make a sound. He must have thought I'd left the store after he heard the doorbell. Crouched on a threadbare Persian rug, I wondered how I was going to make my exit without the door jingling again and without him knowing what I'd overheard. *Think fast*, I told myself, because it was almost five-thirty, and he'd have to come out here to lock up.

My ring! I could open the door, letting the bells jingle, act like I was coming back in, and say I'd changed my mind about getting my diamond ring fixed. By the time he returned to the front, how would he know I hadn't just walked in?

It worked like a charm. "Forget something?" he asked.

I raised my left hand and said, "Changed my mind. I think I will get this ring made smaller, after all." A burning sensation crept from my throat upward. I was a damned lousy liar.

He reached under the counter and brought out a keychain with plain gold rings attached to it, ranging in sizes. He asked, "What size do you take?"

"Six and a half, I think."

"Take off your ring and try this one on."

He separated one of the rings. I slipped it over my knuckle easily, but it seemed loose once it was in place. Feigning concern, I said, "That's the problem, if it's big enough to slide over my knuckle, it twists on my finger."

He offered another ring from the set on the key chain. "Try this one. It's the next size smaller. If you can get it over your knuckle, it'll stay in place better."

I took the ring and slid it onto my finger, but not without difficulty. "How often do you take your rings off? He asked. "To wash dishes? For housework or yard work?"

"Never," I answered.

"This smaller size is fine once you have it on, and if you won't be taking it on and off, a tight fit won't matter." Those piercing ice-blue eyes violated my space again.

"How long will it take?" In fourteen years, I'd never been a day without my ring.

"Couple of days." He had a tablet of receipts, each one with a tear-off end and corresponding number for the customer's claim tag. "Name, address and phone number?"

I gave him the information, took the receipt, and, hurrying out to my truck, breathed a sigh of relief.

The supermarket, in a new strip mall also housing a pharmacy, video rental and Chinese take-out, was my last stop. Our town was bursting at the seams with transplanted city folks and new businesses. Ten years ago, the town consisted of a school, post office, and a feed store. Now, neighborhood kids marched off to one of three schools, and we enjoyed choices of where we bought our groceries and pet food. The post office, however, was unchanged, still crammed into a cute but tiny brick building constructed in the late 1800's. The grip on our small-town sensitivity was loosening, and there was a certain sadness in that.

Grabbing two five-pound bags of carrots, I was headed for the checkout when I heard a familiar voice. "Hey, Carol, why aren't you out riding?"

I spun around. "Lida!" I held up the carrots. "Jack says I should buy stock in a carrot company." She strode, rather than walked, with animation and energy. Dressed in dark paisley silk pants and tan T-shirt with a pattern of horses running across the top, green snakeskin loafers completed her flamboyant jumble of color and texture. "How about you? Doing much riding?" I asked.

"We rode early and enjoyed an absolutely glorious sunrise." She pulled a bit of hay from her chopped salt-and-pepper hair, looked it over, then tossed it down. "You know, Carol, this retirement stuff isn't half bad. A morning ride, lunch, then nap-time. I could get used to it."

"I don't want to hear," I whined. "I'm looking at another twenty years."

"That's if you ever make it to your retirement, with this nut case running loose, bumping people off. Be careful riding."

"I've already been through that issue with Jack, *ad nauseam*." An old man's watery eyes suddenly darted from the tomato sauce cans he examined, to Lida. "Who would kill a sweet girl like Julie?" I asked.

"Some trigger-happy crazed hunter, that's who," she said. "Why on earth they allow hunting on equestrian trails is beyond me. The two don't mix."

"It'll be the horse people that get the boot, if they close it to one and open it exclusively to the other," I said. "If we rock the boat complaining about the hunters, we could lose our trails."

"You're probably right." She shifted from one foot to another. "Going to Julie's service tomorrow?" she asked.

I nodded. "I'm going, but not Jack. He couldn't get the day off; they're short of help again."

Now the geriatric comparative shopper seemed fixated with Lida. Maybe it was the colorful outfit drawing him in, like a crow to a shiny coin. "I'd better run if I'm going to get a ride in before dark," I said.

"On your way out, don't miss the kid running the express lane."

The "twelve items or less" cashier was a teen whose employee tag said, "Hi, my name is Jimmy." Only a blind person could've missed Jimmy's elaborate lime-green hairdo—a nightmare of sculpted and gelled cement-like sections, each piece standing straight out from his head and tipped with a curlicue point, like the twist on a soft-serve ice cream cone. He ran my carrots across the scanner and asked, "Must really like carrots, huh?"

"They're for my horses." I fought the urge to reach out and touch one of the green curls. "Jimmy, I hope you don't mind, but I can't help asking—why the lime-green hair?"

Not offended in the least, he answered without hesitation, "A bunch of us did it to protest dissecting frogs in biology class. There are interactive computer programs and plastic models that teach you the same thing, without making an innocent creature suffer. We wanted dark green to symbolize the green frog, but all the drug store had was lime."

"Did it work? The protest, I mean."

"You bet!" He grinned from ear to ear. "At first they were mad, and hauled us all down to the principal's office and said we had to go home and wash our hair, but after we explained, they agreed to a fund-raiser to buy the computer programs." He dropped my carrots into a paper sack and counted out my change.

"A bake sale?" I asked, my first thoughts always of food.

"Car wash."

"Great! I'll be your first customer. My little Ranger needs a good washing."

The woman behind me plopped a carton of milk and a loaf of bread down, chiming in, "And I'll be your second."

"I got a newsletter from an animal rights organization that said they help fund the cost of dissection alternative programs in schools," I said. I stuffed the change in my wallet. "I'll bring the article in, next time I get groceries."

"Cool! We need all the help we can get. Just write my name on it and drop it off at the manager's office. I'll give it to our biology teacher."

When I got home, I called Marge, first thing. "Want me to stop by for your grocery list?" I asked, trying to sound cheerful, like nothing was wrong.

"No, thanks, I won't be needing anything this week," she said, in a curt, matter-of-fact tone. Then silence.

Damned, stubborn old woman, since when did she go a week without groceries? I wanted to scream at her, but instead, as flat and unemotionally as I could, I said, "Let me know if you need anything between now and Saturday."

"I will," she said and politely hung up the phone.

After leaving Chet's attorney referral on Kathy's answering machine, I changed into riding jeans and a T-shirt sporting a yellow happy face. Mr. Smiley wore a cowboy hat, and proclaimed, "Ya'll have a nice day, now, Podner." Although warm, as soon as the sun slanted low, the evening would get chilly, so I tied a wool jacket around my waist. I grabbed Julie's ring box off the dining room table, where I'd left it next to the mail.

Sound asleep in the open door of his stall, Echo's eyelids drooped, his bottom lip sagging. Unlike Feather, in the paddock contentedly munching grass, after sixteen years as a pampered show horse, Echo preferred lounging indoors. He wanted his meals catered, brought at evenly spaced intervals throughout the day. "Wake up, sleepyhead," I said, dangling a carrot in front of his nose. I put him on the cross-ties for a quick grooming, then saddled up. And because he could be as slow as molasses in January, I strapped on a pair of blunt spurs.

As predicted, we started toward Rene's at a snail's pace. I gently urged him on with my seat, and when that didn't work, drove him forward with my seat *and* legs. But as soon as I relaxed my aching legs, he reverted to tortoise speed again, dilly-dallying and gawking along the way.

When we finally got to Rene's, she was working in her flower bed, her cotton shirt billowing in the breeze. Fringes of dark hair popped out from under the crown of her floppy straw hat. She brushed a tear from her cheek when I held the jewelry box out to her. Neither of us spoke, so I just smiled and turned Echo toward the road, my chest tight and heavy, and an aching lump in my throat.

CHAPTER ELEVEN

"Marge, slow down, I can't understand you." Puddles of water formed at my feet, dripping from the ends of my hair, over my shoulders and down my legs. A trail glistened on the vinyl floor from the bathroom to the phone. Long past eight o'clock, I was expecting it to be Jack. He still wasn't home and I was starting to worry. "From the top, now, what's wrong?"

In between choking and sobbing, she said, "It's Bailey. Oh my God, Carol, it's Bailey! He got into the garbage."

So what? Didn't dogs get into garbage all the time? "Whose garbage?" I asked, in confusion.

"*My* garbage. I think he's eaten *it*. The sauce; you know, *the leftover spaghetti sauce*."

Adrenaline kicked my brain into high gear. What was she saying? Was she admitting she'd poisoned Randy, and now Bailey? Instantly my priorities fell, like dominos, into a line. "Is he breathing? Put your hand beneath his nostrils and tell me if you feel his breath."

"His eyes are fluttering and, yes, I can feel his breath and his sides are going up and down. He was twitching and vomiting, but now he's just laying on his side and I'm not sure… oh, Carol, help me, please. I think he's dying!"

"I just got out of the shower, so I've got to throw some clothes on. I'll be right down. While I'm getting dressed, call Dr. Adler, he won't be there because he's already closed, but the recording will give the phone number of the emergency vet in Pontiac. The twenty-four hour place. Take down the number and call them... tell them we're bringing in a dog that's been poisoned, but it'll take us at least a half hour to get there—maybe longer."

"Please, God,... how could this be happening?"

"They'll need to know what kind of poison it was. You'll have to tell them, Marge."

"I will... I'll tell them."

A twelve-year old Collie wasn't going to make it, unless he'd ingested very little of the poison. I wanted to tell Marge, to set her up for the truth, but instead a voice, clear and strong, called me a quitter, and told me never, never give up, and I wanted to scream, *I don't need your Winston Churchill mentality right now, dad*. And then I knew, if Bailey was breathing at all, if there was the least bit of life left in him, I was going to do my damned best to save him, if I had to break every speed limit from here to the clinic. What happened after that wasn't up to me.

"Have you got a piece of plywood, something flat and solid we can lay him on? An ironing board? No, that's too long." I talked to myself more than Marge. "The table leaf! I know you've got an extension for your dining room table because I've seen it. And we'll need some belts, or rope, or... no, forget it, I'll bring a longe line. My truck is so small, I don't think two of us can fit inside with Bailey, too." I cursed myself again for not getting the club cab. "You still have Roy's truck, don't you? We may have to use it."

"It hasn't been started in over two years and I've let the license plates expire."

"Then mine will have to do." She lapsed into crying again and I quickly said, "Don't worry, we'll get him there. Hang up now and call the clinic, then drag out the table leaf. I'll be right over."

I ran to the closet and tore a pair of jeans and a T-shirt from their hangers. There was no time for underwear or socks and my hair would have to air dry.

Thirty-five minutes later, I felt Bailey's labored breathing on my hand when I dug for the ringing cell phone, pressed between my hip and the crease of the seat. Each rattled exhale told me his lungs were filling with fluid. Marge sat with the mahogany table leaf on her lap, Bailey secured to it by longe line. From the Internet research I'd done, I knew the latter stages of poisoning sometimes produced convulsions and the last thing we needed was an accident caused by his thrashing. The three of us were so crammed into the compact truck we could barely move. I never even suggested putting Bailey in the back, by himself. If he was going to die in my truck, at least he would be with Marge. I flipped open the phone. "Hello?"

"Carol, thank God, you had the phone on. Where are you?"

"In the truck."

"I gathered that much. Where exactly in the truck?"

I peered ahead to the next street sign. "Just past Telegraph and 59. Why?"

"The gun rally went south."

"Jack, I don't need another problem right now. Marge and I are rushing Bailey to the twenty-four hour vet place on Orchard Lake Road." I looked over at Marge's ashen face and worried this was too much for her. *God, please don't let this old lady die on me. Get us all home safe tonight*, I begged. "Bailey's been poisoned."

"Poisoned! By who?"

"Never mind. I'll tell you later." I still didn't know myself, since I hadn't asked Marge and she wasn't volunteering. When the time was right, I'd ask. "But you called *me*, remember? What's up?"

"I'm at the Oakland County Jail."

I groaned. "Tell me you're kidding!" Bailey's eyes rolled back in his head, leaving only the whites showing.

"Unfortunately, I'm not." He lowered his voice, and said, "Matt got us into this, him and his damned big mouth. He's an asshole."

"Tell me something I didn't already know. What are the charges?"

"Just a second, it's written on this citation... Parading without a permit and obstructing traffic and some other legal mumbo-jumbo. Like how much traffic could I obstruct in downtown Ortonville? Give me a break."

"Jack, can't this wait? We're pulling into the clinic."

"As a matter of fact, it can't! I need two hundred dollars to get outta' here."

"I'll have to call you back."

"Carol, you can't call me back—I'm in jail and I need two hundred dollars!"

"I heard you. I'll get the money as soon as I can. Gotta' go."

Ramming the curb, I threw my truck into park, and jumped out to help Marge. I carried one end of Bailey's litter, walking backwards, while a woman in a white lab coat and slacks held the glass doors open. "I'm Dr. Garr," she said, pointing down the hall, "Last room on the left.

We've got an IV set up." Marge's crepe-soled shoes squeaked with each step down the narrow hallway.

Dr. Garr introduced us to a young woman holding a clipboard and scrawling notes. "This is my vet tech, Pam Ashton, she'll get information while I make an exam." Pam glanced from me to Marge. "Who's the dog's owner?"

"I am," Marge said, lifting her eyes only briefly from Bailey.

Pam took down Marge's name and address, then asked, "Purebred Collie?"

Marge nodded.

"Age?"

"Twelve." Pam's eyebrows raised almost imperceptibly, though I was certain Marge missed it. She was focused on Bailey.

Dr. Garr worked deftly, untying Bailey and sliding him onto the stainless steel table. She pulled one eyelid back, drawing a pen light forward and backward and from side to side. "He's not totally blind," she said, "he's got some reactive eye movement." She noted the capillary refill of his gums and listened to his heartbeat. Bailey, as limp as an old rag, offered no resistance, not even when she slid the needle into the vein inside his right front leg. "I'm introducing an IV catheter, balanced electrolytes." Then she rattled off Bailey's vital statistics, while Pam's pen hurriedly scratched. The wall clock said nine-twenty, almost an hour since Marge's call to me at home. I wondered how much time Bailey had.

"As quickly as you can," Dr. Garr said, "Tell me what was in the garbage, what were his symptoms, and how soon they occurred."

"It was leftover spaghetti sauce with mushrooms," Marge said. Her trembling hand pushed a white curl from her face. "Last Sunday, a friend picked mushrooms in the woods. We usually had dinner together on Sunday evenings, and since I was planning spaghetti anyway, he suggested steaming the mushrooms and adding them to the sauce."

Of course! Why hadn't I thought of it? Something finally made sense. I saw Marge's mahogany dinner table set with her elegant white china. I felt her crisp linen napkins. I saw the innocent-looking bowl of steamed morels, only these were false morels—deadly impostors. But I could *not* see Randy in life and I could *not* understand this relationship he had with Marge.

"I've always hated mushrooms from the time I was a little girl and I knew I wouldn't eat any," Marge continued, "so I kept them separate, for Randy." Tears dripped from her cheeks and fell onto Bailey's silky coat, on his shoulder, where a patch of black turned to fawn.

"It was an accident, I swear it, an accident!" she exclaimed.

"We know it was," I said, hurt that she hadn't confided in me, until I remembered almost accusing her of mercy killing.

"Who's Randy?" Dr. Garr asked, confused.

"The friend who picked the mushrooms," I answered.

Marge went on, "Then Randy died and when the Sheriff called, saying he wanted to stop by, I panicked and threw both the sauce and the mushrooms in the garbage, never dreaming in a million years this would happen." She scratched gently behind Bailey's ear. "I give him plenty of dog food, why would he want garbage?"

"It's just one of those things dogs do," Dr. Garr said quietly. "What were the first symptoms you noticed?"

"He was thrashing about, acting crazy, and when I saw the torn plastic trash bag and the mess, I knew what he'd done. At first there was a foamy saliva coming from his mouth, then he began vomiting and all the while, having spasms and twitching." She pointed to me and said, "About that time, I called Carol. After that, he simply went limp."

"What kind of mushrooms were they?" Pam asked.

"Early false morels," I piped up. "Randy died at Pontiac General, where they did an autopsy. The poison was called…" I tugged the ends of my hair, trying to think, but I was all muddled up and couldn't remember the chemical name. "Something with the initials 'MM,' mono-something."

"MMH?" Dr. Garr asked.

"That's it, MMH!"

"Monomethylhydrazine," Dr. Garr said to Pam. "Get on the Michigan State poison hotline. Have Donna call pathology at Pontiac General. Ask what they used to counteract the poison. It may have been pyridoxine and vitamin K, or possibly charcoal. Hydrazines attack the liver, so I'll run LDH, SGOT and bilirubin levels."

Dr. Garr said to Marge, "I'm going to draw blood and run tests that'll tell us what's happening to his internal organs, his kidneys and heart, but especially his liver. In the meantime, stay here with him. Pet him and speak to him softly, trying to keep his attention." She smiled, "How long have you had him?"

"Since he was a puppy," Marge answered, stroking his long, slender nose.

"We'll continue the intravenous feeding while we run the tests. As soon as we've spoken with the university and have the blood chemistry, we'll outline your options." She placed her hand gently on Marge's wrist. "To be honest, though, a twelve-year-old Collie is a senior citizen. His condition is extremely guarded, at best, and the symptoms you've mentioned, the twitching and thrashing, signal neurological damage, which is irreversible. I'm sorry, I wish I could give you more hope." She filled a purple-stoppered vial with Bailey's blood, then hurried away.

We were alone in the room now and, crying, Marge buried her face in Bailey's soft, long hair. This was not the tough old bird I knew, the one who never cried, not even at her husband's funeral. Feeling awkward and not knowing how else to comfort her, I hugged her trembling shoulders. Bailey never moved. His eyes rolled back, wild and cock-eyed, at odd angles.

"It was an accident," I said again. However inadequate, it was all I could think of. With our silence, the ticking of the wall clock became deafening, ticking the minutes of Bailey's life away.

Then I thought of Jack, sitting in a jail cell, waiting for me. I couldn't leave Marge now; I had to stay with her, at least until we heard back from the university. Maybe if I called Denise, she could go get him, except I had the Visa card and he needed money, so that wouldn't work. Pam's voice carried down the hall, "State says gastric lavage one to four hundred tannic acid, one to five thousand potassium permanganate *or* activated charcoal. General used potassium."

I peeked into the hall. Dr. Garr sat at the counter along the back wall, her shoulders hunched over a microscope.

"Liver's all but shut down. Not surprising. We could try the activated charcoal. Can't do any harm."

I slipped back inside the examining room and prayed they used every power they had to save Bailey. How could Dr. Garr know what Marge had been through, living alone, with no one but the dog to talk to most of the time? He was so much more than a dog, he was her companion, a good friend.

When she came back, Dr. Garr's green eyes probed Marge's. "There's something we can try... gastric lavage of activated charcoal."

"Is that painful—gastric lavage?" Marge asked.

"It's a stomach tube. Not pleasant by any means, but not terribly invasive either. We flush out his stomach with the charcoal, hopefully absorbing the poisons and washing them away. We can try it, it's up to you; but his liver doesn't look good and we're running out of time, so if we do it, we must do it *now*. It's your call."

"What other options are there?"

She was brutally frank. "With it, he has a slim chance—without it, none at all."

Marge didn't hesitate. "Do it."

I'd had horses long enough to remember what stomach tubing an animal was like, back in the days before paste wormer. I needed to get Marge out. "There's a little café next door, Marge, let's grab a cup of coffee. There's nothing more you can do here, for now."

"She's right," Pam said, "Go ahead. We'll stay with him and we know where to find you if anything changes."

Four small booths along one wall and a couple of tables filled the tiny café. The glass case underneath the cash register held mammoth cinnamon buns labeled "bear claws," and reminded me I hadn't eaten dinner.

"Two cups of coffee," I said to the girl. Her black hair cascaded in long waves down her back. Some people had all the luck.

"If you're not in a hurry, I'll make a fresh pot," she said. "This stuff is old."

"Sounds good to me." I gratefully plopped down in a hard metal chair at one of the tables, across from Marge. She looked as beat as I felt and so very frail and tiny.

"I suppose it'd be better if Bailey dies anyway," she said.

"How do you figure that?"

"Who would take care of him? I'm going to prison. I killed Randy."

"Don't be silly. You didn't kill Randy and you're not going to prison. He picked the mushrooms, all you did was cook them." Who on earth was going to prosecute an eighty-year-old woman who mistakenly served poison mushrooms to a friend? Especially when the friend was the one who picked them. "Jack and I did some research on that MMH stuff. Because it acts on the liver, an alcoholic like Randy would react more severely to the poison than would a normal person. So in a way, he killed himself." Then I remembered the part about the age, too, how age can render the liver dysfunctional, and I thought of Bailey. "But, seriously, Bailey might not make it. He's old and this is a big shock to his system. Dr. Garr seems to know what she's doing, but it might be out of her hands."

"I just don't want him to suffer any more."

"They won't let that happen. If it gets to that point, she'll tell you. My experience with veterinarians is that they're lots more honest than medical doctors."

"Is everything all right with Jack?" Marge asked.

I'd forgotten all about him. "My dear, beloved husband is resting his laurels in jail at this very moment."

"Jail! Whatever for?"

"That damned gun rally. I knew there'd be trouble, but does he ever listen to me? Of course not. Anyway, we've got bigger problems right now. I'll get him home somehow. Let's see how Bailey does and then we'll worry about Jack."

"Leave me here and go to Jack. I'll find a way home." This was the Marge I knew.

"And what about Bailey? How are you going to get him home?"

"Jack is your husband! He's got to come first."

"He'll keep. Might do him some good. You know, Sheriff Morton's wracked his brain trying to deal with Julie's murder, then Randy... Oh, my God, Marge, I just realized, somebody's got to tell Sheriff Morton about Randy. The truth, I mean."

If it was possible, she looked even more miserable. "I suppose I've got to face the music sooner or later, though later would suit me fine."

"No sense putting it off." Digging into my purse, I found the crumpled slip of paper with the sheriff's direct number on it. Had it only been Sunday when, mesmerized by his sagging-jowled face, I took the paper he pressed into my hand and promised I'd call with any new information? Sunday seemed eons ago. "The longer you wait, the more explaining you'll have to do. Besides, maybe he can help with Jack." I stood on achy legs. "The cell phone's in the truck."

Stepping into the cool night air, the city surrounded me in its blanket of muffled, yet ever present, din of traffic, its flashing neon signs and the smell of fried food. Had I lived in the country long enough for this to become alien? I heard not a single cricket.

"Morton here."

"Sheriff, it's Carol Ward. Sorry to call so late, but something's come up. About Randy." Silence told me he needed refreshing. "You know, the poisoning case?"

"Yeah, sure, Carol, what's up?"

"It was an accident."

"What was an accident?"

"The whole thing. His death." Maybe I was so tired I only made sense to myself. "Marge accidentally poisoned him with homemade spaghetti sauce. Randy picked the mushrooms and gave them to her to cook. I guess they ate dinner together on Sunday nights. Talk about unlikely dinner partners."

"How do you know all this?"

"Because she threw the mushrooms in the garbage and her old dog got into it. We're at the vet's right now but I don't think he's going to make it. Anyway, she painted herself into a corner and had to come clean for the sake of the dog."

"Why'd she lie to me?"

"She didn't really lie; she just didn't tell you everything. Can you cut her some slack on this? She's eighty years old and terrified. She thinks she's going to prison."

"Serve her right. Withholding evidence."

"C'mon, you don't mean that. Think of her as somebody's nice old grandma, baking cookies."

"Yeah, poisonous cookies. I'll have to talk to her again. Can you bring her in?"

"Well, that's the problem, my husband's in jail and I'm here with Marge and this sick dog."

"Jail? What'd he do now? Wait, don't tell me... he was with the NRA group they brought in?"

"How'd you guess?"

"I'm just lucky." He let out a long sigh. "I wish like hell I'd gone on vacation this week, wished I was anywhere but here. Gun rallies, shootings, old ladies poisoning people, I've had enough trouble in that one-horse town in the past week to last me a lifetime."

I ignored his tirade, figuring he was entitled. "And robbery."

"What?"

"You forgot the robberies."

"Yeah, right, those too."

"Like I said, I'm here with Marge and the dog, and we're waiting for the vet to try some treatment and Jack says he needs two hundred dollars and the thing is, I've got the Visa card and I can't really leave Marge right now."

"All right, all right. I'll call in and see what I can do. I'm headed to my place in an hour or so, I'll drop Jack home on my way."

"Thank you, thank you, thank you! A million thank you's!" With a paunch like his, I figured Sheriff Morton's hobby was eating, like some people jog or collect stamps. "How about I make you a batch of chocolate chip cookies?"

"Yeah, right. Straight from hell's kitchen to my lips, baked by the Angels of Death? I think not."

Dr. Garr leaned over Bailey, her stethoscope pressed against his heart. I noticed his eyes were still now, quiet and clouded with milkiness. "His eyes aren't darting all over anymore," I said with hope.

Dr. Garr pulled her stethoscope from her ears, straightening up. Her white lab coat crinkled, stiff and rough with starch, when she moved. "Actually, that's not an improvement. We aren't getting any eye response at all."

"Maybe the charcoal hasn't had enough time?" I asked.

"In the past half hour, we've watched respiration and heartbeat steadily decline, which is the opposite of what we want. Everything signals a coma. The magnitude of the liver damage is just too great for an old dog."

"Is it time to let him go?" Marge's clear voice asked, without a hint of a quiver or a crack.

"Afraid so," Dr. Garr said. "We've done all we can. More would only prolong his suffering and wouldn't be fair to either you or him."

"Then do what you have to," Marge said. "But first, can I spend a minute alone with him?"

She laid her hand over Marge's, her long slender fingers curled slightly. "Take all the time you want."

Dr. Garr and I stepped into the narrow hall and she closed the door. She whispered, "I feel so bad for her, I really did all I could."

"I know, and Marge knows, too. This week has been a nightmare for her, first the neighbor girl, then her friend, now her dog. She's a widow; the dog was all she had." I leaned back, resting my shoulder against the wall. "Do you have something we can wrap him in? I know she'll want to bury him at home."

They say death always comes in threes. Tomorrow we would bury a young woman, an old man, and a faithful friend.

CHAPTER TWELVE

Rain pelted the house and dripped from the lilacs brushing my bedroom window. Jack's pillow, long cold, held the indentation where it cradled his head. I vaguely remembered him padding through the bedroom at dawn.

I made coffee, then dialed Marge's number. "Jack take care of everything?" I asked. With the phone tucked between chin and shoulder, I warmed my hands on the steaming coffee mug.

"Bless his heart," she said. "He made a pine-board coffin, and lined it with the cedar from Bailey's bed. He just left, said he had to be to work by nine."

Shivering, though I wore both a sweatshirt and T-shirt, I thought of Jack digging Bailey's grave in the cold spring rain. "Randy's service is at nine-thirty and Julie's is at eleven-thirty. I'd be glad to give you a lift, if you're up to going." Through unspoken terms, Bailey's dying had brought us back together.

"That'd be nice. What a godforsaken day, pouring rain and as black as night. Not even during the war did I bury three people in one day."

I wasn't about to remind her Bailey wasn't a person. "Are you sure both funerals won't be too much, considering you were up half the night? I'd be glad to bring you home in-between."

"I don't want to be any trouble."

"Marge, it's only three miles. I can run you home and be back in plenty of time for Julie's funeral."

She hesitated. "If you're staying for both, I'll stay too."

I knew she was exhausted. "It's no trouble. Honest." I waited. "Tell you what—don't decide now. After Randy's Mass, see how you feel."

When I picked her up, I saw the mound of fresh black dirt and the wooden cross Jack had made for Bailey. Randy's service was a small, quiet affair, and afterwards Marge agreed she was done in, and would rather be taken home. Julie's funeral, by contrast, was packed with neighbors and members of the equestrian club, her friends from school, Rene's students. And somewhere there were reporters, too, because a Detroit News van was parked in the lot.

I waved to Ann, owner of Tack Full, the saddle shop in town. Lida and her husband, Perry, sat three rows back from Ron, and Lida motioned to me that she'd saved me a seat. I pointed to the front, where Rene stood before the casket, her back to the crowd, and Lida nodded.

I went up to Rene and put my arm around her. The absence of flowers and the stark, flawless beauty of the closed coffin startled me. I ran my fingers across its smooth mahogany finish.

"Julie wouldn't pick flowers in the summer," she said. "She didn't want them to die. That's why I asked for donations to the humane society instead of flowers."

"She's smiling on you," I said. "She'll always be smiling on you."

Rene turned to me. Her voice was flat, emotionless, and she spoke slowly, as if fighting for control. "This is all wrong." Her lip quivered. "Parents aren't supposed to bury their kids."

"You're right, it *is* all wrong, Rene, but not because it was her and not you," I said. "Because it's wrong for someone to snuff out another's life." She didn't seem to hear.

"Less than a week ago, I worried about who she dated, and if he was good enough for her. It seemed so important at the time." A tear traveled a jagged path down her face.

Taking her hand in mine, I said, "We can't predict what will happen to us or to those we love."

She looked into my eyes with a sudden intensity, and said, "Now I know, Carol, that you've got to love the people around you every single day. You've got to cherish every moment spent with them, because that may be all you've got."

In the quiet funeral home, the Pastor's black suit rustled as he and Ron walked toward us.

"Let's sit down, hon, he's ready to start," Ron said, taking Rene's hand and leading her away. Beads of sweat glistened on his forehead.

I slid into the seat next to Lida, who fanned herself with a prayer card. "It's sweltering in here," she whispered.

"I guess I didn't notice until now, but yeah, you're right," I said, loosening the silk scarf I wore around my neck. I leaned closer to Lida. "I took Marge home. She's worn to a frazzle."

"The past week has been an absolute nightmare."

"That's an understatement," I said.

An hour later, we filtered into the parking lot, a somber, rain-coated group. Thankful to be outside, leaving behind the stuffy mixture of designer perfumes, I felt a sinus headache coming on.

"Can I bum a ride with you?" Lida asked. "Perry's not staying for the burial or the luncheon. He's got an appointment with a builder."

"Sure." I unlocked the passenger-side door of my truck. Mildly curious, I asked, "What's he building?"

"I forgot to tell you?"

Lida was forever forgetting to tell me things. "Tell me what?" I asked.

"In Monday's downpour, the roof of the chicken coop caved in."

"Just like that?" I snapped my fingers. "It fell right in?"

"Everything's ruined! Nesting boxes, roosts, a colossal mess!" She got in and slammed the door.

I walked around and unlocked my side. "Where've you put the chickens?"

"We rented a canvas party tent, but we're being charged by the day, and it's costing a small fortune."

I sensed the direction this was taking. "I'd love to help, really I would, but with so many cats, I don't know." I heard myself telling Jack sixty-seven chickens were temporarily moving in with us. "It just wouldn't work."

"I understand. Perry always said our place was a three-ring circus, I guess the tent just makes it complete." Lowering her voice, even though it was only her and I inside my truck, she said, "I wonder how Rene feels about Derrick being here. He was brought in for questioning."

"They questioned a lot of people," I said. "I imagine at first, anyone is considered a suspect, maybe even Denise and I, because we found Julie."

"I heard he wanted to date her, but she wouldn't go out with him."

"When did you hear that?" I asked, wondering how Lida got these tidbits.

"Last Saturday, at Tack Full. I was picking up my old hunting saddle."

"That ancient Passier?"

"Yes, the ancient Passier," she mimicked my voice.

"I can't believe you've still got that old thing," I said, wondering what this had to do with anything. Lida's conversations had an easy way of derailing.

"The trouble with you, Carol, is you have no appreciation for fine, old things."

"What needed fixing now?" I asked.

"Nothing, I just had it restuffed." She flashed me a quick, hot look, begging me to differ.

I didn't. Old leather needed constant care and repair, and Lida's tack was hand-me-downs from her grandfather. The fox hunting gene skipped a generation and resurfaced in Lida.

"Ann sent it out and called last week to say it was done. While I was browsing the store, Kathy came in and I overheard their conversation."

The funeral director walked the line-up of vehicles, thumping an orange magnetic-based flag to each one. I pulled the headlight switch. "Not consenting to a date is hardly a reason to kill someone." Was I defending him?

"You've got to admit he doesn't exactly have a great track record."

"He may be a thief, but murder? Besides, would he show up here today if he had something to hide?" I asked.

"There have been cases where model citizens ended up convicted killers. What about what's-his-name, the one who killed college girls? And the other guy that only killed women after a rainstorm."

We both glanced outside, at the black clouds. "I suppose it's possible. I suppose *anything's* possible," I said.

Our umbrellas formed a circle around Julie's grave, where we stood on a hill, little muddy rivers flowing under our waterlogged shoes. I heard traffic passing by on the wet pavement below.

Afterward, we were invited to a luncheon at the closest restaurant with banquet facilities. Lida and I joined Kathy, Denise and Derrick at their table. Glad to get in out of the rain, we drank coffee that was neither hot enough nor strong enough.

"I hear they'll be spraying the park for gypsy moths," I said, hoping to spark a conversation.

"We finally got the go-ahead from the environmentalists. It should've been done long before now," Kathy said. She stirred three huge spoonfuls of sugar into coffee that was pale with half and half. I wondered what her secret to staying slim was.

Denise spoke up. "I don't think they should use helicopters; it'll scare half the wildlife out of the park, not to mention coating nearby houses with chemicals."

"Do we have a choice?" Kathy asked. "We've got to dust the tops of the trees. What do you want me to do, run around with spray cans and do all four thousand acres myself?" Red crept up her neck and into her face.

"Mom, it's nothing personal," Derrick interjected, "She's just concerned about the animals, that's all."

"No, she's not! It's her precious flower beds she's worried about!" Kathy stood up, towering over Denise. "It may be the only thing that saves your flower beds, or any of your trees, for that matter."

I looked to Lida, silently pleading she do something, but she raised her eyebrows and said nothing.

"It's the homes and the people living in them that I'm concerned about." Denise's eyes lowered. "In case you forgot, we've already got one member of the family dying of cancer."

"It's a perfectly safe chemical," Kathy said.

"Safe like fluoride was in the water systems in the sixties? And asbestos and x-rays?" Denise stood, her eyes glaring into Kathy's. "If it's so safe, why isn't it being sprayed anywhere near the ranger station? Have *your* house dusted."

Lida and I looked at each other in disbelief.

"That does it—Derrick, let's go. I don't have to listen to this! Next she'll be blaming me for the earthquakes in California." Kathy grabbed her purse from the table.

Derrick stood to go, glancing between us and his mother, who was already at the door, pulling on her coat. "I'm sorry. She's upset, about, well, just about everything, right now," he stammered, and went after his mom.

Turning to Denise, I felt heat rising in my face. "I'm sorry, I didn't mean to start trouble. I had no idea…"

She yanked her coat from her chair and pointed her umbrella at me. "For once in your life, Carol Ward, why don't you just shut up!" Tears rolled down her cheeks. She pushed her chair in and left the restaurant.

Open-mouthed, I watched her go.

"I'll say one thing, Carol, you sure know how to start a conversation," Lida said.

Rene came over to our now empty table, "What's up with those two?"

"They're fighting over gypsy moths," I said.

"Gypsy moths? What started that?" Rene asked.

"Carol didn't realize it was such a controversial subject," Lida said. "The township and the state have been arguing with the environmentalists for years. They finally got the okay."

"It sounded like a good thing in the newspaper," I said defensively.

Rene smiled, the first I'd seen from her in a while. The earthen tones she wore complemented her warm complexion and dark hair. "First rule of thumb, Carol, don't believe everything you read in the newspaper."

When it was time to go, Lida and I stood under the restaurant's yellow canopy. "Wait here," I told her, pulling my raincoat tight. "I'll get the truck. No sense in both of us getting soaked."

"Must be monsoon season," she said.

We drove in an easy silence, rain cascading down the windshield. When I turned off the main highway, I said, "Everything looks so green and alive, I love springtime. Even in a downpour."

"This sure has been a spring to remember," she said. "On second thought, maybe it's one we should try to forget."

I pulled into Lida'a gravel drive and slowly rumbled across her one-lane wooden bridge. The blue and white-striped party tent, nearly the size of my horse barn, was adjacent to her pasture. Chickens meandered everywhere. They took up residence on the porch, under the carport, some explored the aisle of the stable. And in a heap lay the demolished coop.

"My beautiful coop," she sighed, "I'm just sick over it."

I shivered in the damp chill, surveying the damage. A tarp had been thrown up, presumably to cover the collapsed roof, but the wind had blown it over itself and rain was running inside, on the blue painted roosts.

"Come inside for a glass of wine," she said.

I hung up my coat while she put an armful of wood into the fireplace. "What a day," she said. She crumpled a newspaper, threw it on top of the wood and lit a match to it. "Funerals are bad enough, without ending up in the middle of a feud."

"Honestly, I had no idea what I was getting into." Lida opened the French doors overlooking the terrace. Rain dripped from the fringe of the patio umbrella. "I was trying to *avoid* trouble by averting attention from the investigation or the fact Derrick is a suspect. Do you honestly think he had anything to do with it?"

"I don't know. I just can't believe he'd do something like that." She disappeared into the kitchen.

"And if he did, would he come to the funeral?" I called to her. Lida's big gray tom cat sniffed my pant leg, and apparently reaching the conclusion that I was trustworthy, hopped into my lap. "This must be awful for Kathy. She's got to know what everybody is wondering."

"That's what's got her on edge; I'd lay money on it," Lida said. "I've never known her to be so nasty. She's terrified of what Derrick may be mixed up in. She can't control him—never has been able to, and it's driving her crazy." She poured white wine into two goblets and set the bottle on the end table between us.

"Denise wasn't much better," I said. "She's usually so polite it's annoying."

"You and I say things like that to each other all the time and nobody gets upset. But then, we've been through a lot over the years."

The fire crackled and hissed and seemed to pull dampness from the air. "Remember when we got lost riding through that swamp?" I asked.

"And that was *after* we scrambled through those briars, getting torn and scratched from head to toe," Lida laughed. "When we finally came out in that field of goldenrod and I saw the houses and the road, I could've cried!"

"Remember when we went to the movies and the seat of your chair fell through? I laughed so hard I thought I was going to be sick."

"And the man in the row behind us complained."

We were still giggling when Perry brought in the newspaper. "The Pontiac police raided a pawn shop and recovered stolen electronics from last Friday's break-in," he read from the front page. "There's a composite sketch of the guy who brought them in."

"Anybody we know?" Lida asked.

"Don't think so," he said, holding the paper up for her to see. "He's in custody, but he's a minor and his name is being withheld."

"Anything new about the murder investigation?" I asked.

"Some people that camped over by the lake are being questioned." He seemed nervous, flipping his key chain back and forth, almost as if there was something more he wanted to say.

"I hope this doesn't end up being one of those long, dragged-out and unsolved cases," Lida said. "Glass of wine, Perry?"

He rubbed his hands together, warming them. "Don't mind if I do."

"We were just reliving old times when you came in. Did you get my opal ring?" Lida asked over her shoulder, on her way into the kitchen.

"It's not ready yet. I told him you'd be by next week."

"What opal ring?" I asked.

"My anniversary gift," Lida called from the kitchen. "Our fortieth is next week. Wait until you see it, it's absolutely gorgeous." She came back with a goblet for Perry.

"I've got something in the truck I don't think you'll be quite as enthusiastic about, but I didn't know what else to do with them," Perry said.

"Them?" Lida asked.

Perry looked sheepishly at his shoes.

"In forty years, I've learned one thing, and that's when you get that look, I get nervous," Lida said.

"Wait here," he said.

We looked at each other quizzically, grabbed our coats and followed him out the door. I threw my hood over my head against the rain. On the seat of the big pick-up was an air conditioner box.

"You bought an air conditioner?" Lida asked, confused, the shoulders of her coat pulled up over her head. "You're right, I'm not enthusiastic about an air conditioner in April. Try me in July."

He opened one of the corner flaps on the box. A black furry head poked out, and then another, except the second one had a patch of white across its nose.

"Kittens?" Lida screeched.

Two round-eyed faces peered out of the box. "Look how cute they are!" I said, lifting one out and tucking it inside my coat.

"Someone abandoned them at the lumberyard and it was time for them to lock up. They were going to put the box out in the rain." He finally looked up, at Lida. "I couldn't leave them," he said.

"Of course you couldn't," I said.

"My husband, the soft-hearted one," Lida smiled. "What are *we* going to do with them?"

"Don't look at me," I said. "I've got too many already." The little ball of fur I held wasn't much bigger than the palm of my hand. A small pink mouth opened, but nothing except a squeak came out. With such tiny white teeth, I wondered if they could even eat soft food yet. "They might need bottle feeding."

Lida groaned.

"Wait a minute!" I said, putting the kitten back in the box. "I just thought of somebody who needs these guys."

"*Needs* them? Like who?" Lida asked in disbelief.

"Marge. Without Bailey, she's sitting in that big house, all alone, and she hardly ever goes anywhere. Who could be a better candidate? She's got the time to bottle feed them. It might be the best thing for her right now."

I transferred the box to my Ranger, started the truck and turned the heater on, full blast, to keep the kittens warm. "My purse is inside." I jumped the steps of the wooden deck and grabbed it off the end table. Perry and Lida waited by the truck, watching the kittens. "I'll take them to Marge's right now."

I drove out the driveway, and suddenly, alone in my truck, the solemnness of the day, its funerals, its tears, and all its finality, hit me. I wanted this moment to last infinitely, to grip onto life today and clutch it tightly in my hand, protected, safe, everything and everyone forever unchanged, and I knew, with an aching sadness, how impossible that was. Life changes with each second. We are already different persons than we were yesterday. Someday I would lose Perry and Lida and Marge, and Jack too, or they would lose me, and there wasn't a damn thing anyone could do about it.

CHAPTER THIRTEEN

I dreamed someone tried to breathe life into an anemic engine. The starter chugged, over and over, but refused to catch, and soon the grinding came slower and slower, until it finally stopped and peaceful silence reigned.

"You up?"

Startled, I opened my eyes. A weak gray light filtered through the blinds. "I am now," I said. Jack towered over me, mountainous, in blue jeans and canvas jacket, holding a paper lunch sack.

"Can I take your truck? It rained all night and mine won't start."

I dragged myself onto one elbow and must not have looked like I'd be coherent anytime soon, because he didn't wait for my answer. "C'mon, hon, I've got to go; I'm running late."

Still confused, I asked, "What day is it?"

"Saturday." A disgusted look told me time was wasting. "Do you need your truck today?"

"Saturday," I said, falling back onto my pillow. Saturday was supermarket day. "Just for groceries. We can get by until tomorrow. If I get desperate, I'll call Denise or Lida."

"Keys?"

I pointed to the dresser, where I'd tossed them last night. "Next to my purse," I said, but he was rummaging through a stack of bills. "Don't mess those up, they're all sorted."

He tossed the keys up and caught them. "Call me later. There's something I want to tell you, but I don't have time now."

He was gone before I had a chance to say good-bye, so I pulled the warm blankets up to my shoulders, hoping to fall back asleep, but the spell was broken, I was awake. The digital clock display said seven forty-five. Yes, he *was* going to be late. I tried to remember how much gas the truck had in it. Hopefully enough for him to make it.

I stumbled into the kitchen for a cup of coffee. The cats, in their infinite quest for entertainment, had found the ball of waxed thread I left on the dining room table (a reminder to myself to redo the slobber straps on Echo's reins) and used it to tether the legs of the dining room table and all four chairs together.

The weather report wasn't pretty. A line of thunderstorms was moving in, so if I wanted to ride, I'd better do it now, before afternoon.

I grabbed jeans and sweatshirt, clean underwear and socks, and along with my coffee, headed for the shower. The hot water felt good, loosening my stiff joints. Why I bothered to blow dry my hair, when it would soon be squashed flat, into the style known as helmet head, was one of the great mysteries of life, but I did it anyway. After I dressed I gave Jack a call.

"Did you make it on time?" I asked. An electric saw whined in the background.

"Of course not. A cup of gas is not enough to make it to Clarkston."

I changed the subject, "So what's up? You had something you wanted to tell me."

"This morning's news said some guy is missing. His wife says he left, on foot, a week ago. Apparently he lost his job, he's been despondent and has nasty anxiety attacks. They live over there by Todd and Denise. His wife thinks he's staying somewhere in the woods."

"Great. Just what we need—another looney tune on the loose."

"She knows he's got a gun. It's possible he shot Julie."

"But why?"

"Maybe he's taking pot shots at random, who knows? The wife says he uses cocaine."

"It just gets better and better, doesn't it? An anxious despondent who uses cocaine and carries a gun," I said sarcastically.

"Now do you have enough reason to stay out of the woods?"

He wasn't going to goad me. "Do you remember why we chose to stay in the country?"

"Peace and quiet."

"Tranquillity and ambiance. The beauty of the natural world. No one's going to take that away from me."

"Why do you have to be so damned stubborn?"

"It's not stubbornness, it's a refusal to cower to the media hype." I remembered what Rene said about the newspapers. "We don't know if any of this is fact."

"You just won't listen, will you?"

I steered the conversation another direction. "Speaking of ambiance, did you see the cats' mixed media creation?"

"The string art project, involving the dining room chairs?" he asked. "Have you unwound them?"

"It's on my list."

"I've got a customer," he said abruptly. "Keep the doors locked and if you ride, stay on the road."

Riding on the road was almost as boring as riding in an arena, except the horse went in a straight line instead of circles. There was no way I was agreeing to that. "I'll be careful," I said.

The stable floor was slick with rain. I'd left the back door open last night, with just the bars across fitted into the slats, to hold the horses in. Halters and lead ropes lay in a heap on the floor, where the wind had blown them off their hooks.

Feather and Echo, munching wet grass in the back pasture, lifted their heads when I shook feed buckets, rattling a mixture of sweet feed, pellets and alfalfa cubes. They thundered in, stopping on a dime within feet of my side, Echo nosing his bucket greedily. Then I led them to their stalls and tossed each a flake of hay.

A gust of wind blew the big sliding door back on me when I struggled to close it. My hair whipped around my face, stinging my eyes. If this wind kept up, it was only a matter of time before a tree came down on a power line and we lost electricity.

Inside, the house seemed unnaturally quiet and calm, out of the howling wind. In the time I had to kill while the horses ate, I put on a Bob Dylan CD, started a load of laundry and began my weekly housecleaning ritual. An hour and a half later, when the dryer buzzer sounded, I heaved the mound of warm clothes onto the bed. Camille burrowed into the fresh laundry, kneading her toes and purring. I grabbed my raincoat and stepped onto the deck, praising myself for remembering to lock the back door.

Feather was groomed and saddled in a half hour. The back roads were deeply rutted where four-wheel drives had passed through since yesterday's rain. Standing water filled the wide tire grooves. Feather balanced herself on the center of the two-track, keeping her feet dry.

On Blood Road, we picked up a rocking-horse canter for the short distance to the trail leading into the Tamaracks. I slowed her to a walk and she picked her way gingerly up the eroded hill. In the woods, sheltered by the trees, the cool air was damp and still.

At the top of the hill was an oak tree with a branch that formed a perfect right angle. It was here that a couple weeks ago, in the early evening, a barred owl crossed my path in an enormous blur of gray, white and brown feathers. He settled in a hollowed-out hole in the elbow of the tree, his eyes, fierce dark orbs, meeting mine.

I tried to see if he was nested in the cubbyhole now; it was late morning and I knew they hunted by night. Something caught my eye in the nook, something darker than the rough bark, but thick brambles surrounding the massive oak kept me from getting close enough to see. Dismounting, I coaxed Feather through the brambles, the thorny brush tearing at my jeans and drawing blood to my hands. I pushed the thin branches aside, bending them one way or the other, making a path down the middle. I guessed the hidey-hole to be about eleven feet up. From where I stood whatever it was looked smooth and rectangular. My heart leapt to my throat. It was so simple, why hadn't I thought to look here sooner?

The tape recorder was in the crook of the tree!

There was a low branch, which I thought would support my weight, and if I got a foothold, maybe I could boost myself within reach of the hollow. I figured that was how Julie had done it. *Only I'm not nineteen years old*, I told myself, and it's been a long time since I climbed a tree. Just how was I going to get the thing down?

My dad's voice, and his inventive, stubborn Yankee ingenuity told me *stop, think, there's always a way. Break a task into its smallest components, and put them in order.*

What's the first thing I need to do? I asked myself. Add five feet to my height, was the answer.

I had a germ of a plan. Feather is just over five feet high at the withers, I thought. If I stood on the saddle, and coupled her five feet with my five and a half feet, I could reach into the hole. The trick would be to position Feather and convince her to stand still.

I climbed back into the saddle. Laying the reins on her neck, every time I reached one knee up to the pommel, she began walking away. I firmly stopped her each time and told her to stand, hoping somehow she understood. I tried it again, this time holding the leather reins in my teeth, tasting a salty mixture of dried sweat and saddle soap. Once again she moved off and I tucked my chin into my chest to tighten the reins.

"Whoa," I said, through clenched teeth, and she stopped. Awkwardly, I reached my other knee up onto the pommel, praying she didn't spook. Now I was balanced in a kneeling position on the seat of the saddle.

I needed something to reassure her, something to keep her standing quietly while I performed my balancing act. From my horse show days, I remembered humming to settle our nerves, both hers and mine. Silent Night was the first thing that came to mind and when I began humming, her ears flicked back toward me. It was working; she was listening! Slowly raising one knee, I teetered, and placed my foot on the saddle. Leaning my right hand, the one closest to the hollow cavity, against the tree for support, I set my other foot on the saddle. I was standing! Now to reach up and grab the recorder.

The smooth plastic case of the recorder was covered with crusted bird droppings. With my hand around it, I slid it forward, but it scraped against the tree, startling Feather, and she lurched forward. My feet fell out from under me, my back thudded painfully hard onto the cantle of the saddle, and I slid along Feather's flank to the ground, landing on my feet and still holding the recorder. Feather moved ahead several yards, stopping to crop tall grass.

"Whoa, girl, that's a good girl," I spoke softly, as I walked toward her. She let me reach for the reins, looped over her neck. I tried to squeeze the recorder into one of the pockets on the saddle pad, but the pouch was too small, and one end stuck out of the top. "It's a tight fit," I told Feather, "but it should make it home."

My left foot was in the stirrup, pulling myself up, when I heard rustling in the brush behind me. A hand roughly grabbed Feather's rein from my grip. In a blur, Feather violently jerked backward against the bit and sent the intruder sprawling. Her thrust threw me awkwardly into the saddle before she reeled and I screamed. My left foot came free of the stirrup.

Badly unseated, for an instant I thought I was going to fall off. Then I clamped my legs around Feather's sides and regained my seat, catching a glimpse of black jeans and a dark bomber-style jacket. An orange ski cap hid face and hair. I pressed my heels into Feather's sides with as much strength as I could muster and she surged forward, lightning fast. Both stirrups banged her sides.

We flew down the trail, Feather jumping the gnarled roots of the Tamaracks in one steep, downhill leap. Sand crumbled beneath her pounding hooves. I felt for the stirrups and slid them onto my feet.

The power beneath me was exhilarating. The rhythm of her gallop shot through me as her huge strides effortlessly rocketed us across the ground and the wind whistled in my ears. Downed logs in the trail loomed ahead, then fell below and finally, behind, as we sailed over them like a leaf floating on an autumn breeze.

In a full galloping position, I held my head low, along the left side of her neck. Low branches slapped against my helmet with loud thumps. I turned my head, lowering my eyes to look underneath my arm, to see the tape recorder still in the pocket of the saddle pad.

Feather was blowing hard, in synch with each stride, white foamy sweat clinging by clumps to her neck and the reins. Almost out of the pines now, I wanted to pull her up, but I didn't dare stop until we got to the county road, just the other side of the sandy ditch.

She jumped the ditch, then lunged up the bank, onto the gravel road. No sooner had we reached the road, when she spooked, her ears pricked toward the opposite side of the road. Nestled in the maples next to the shoulder, was a black Harley-Davidson motorcycle.

When we reached the gouged clay tire grooves, I slowed her to a walk, then turned through the meadow, letting her pick her way through the tall grass.

Looking behind for any sign of the motorcycle, I felt safer the nearer we got to houses, and though most of them appeared deserted, I could quickly duck into a driveway if I had to. For the first time I realized I was drenched in a cold sweat. On top of everything else, black storm clouds were rolling in alarmingly fast from the west.

My head was jammed with unanswered questions. If my attacker wanted the recorder, he must be the murderer, or somehow involved. I needed a plan of action, I told myself, the first thing being to call the police. But what was I going to say? Sure, I had the tape recorder, but what could I tell them about my would-be assailant? I wasn't sure of anything. I never saw a face or heard a voice, and in jeans and a short jacket, I couldn't even be positive it was a man.

Secondly, I needed to hide Feather. Whoever jumped us in the woods could identify me through her, and there was only one bright red chestnut in this neighborhood. If only she were a bay. There are lots of bays around here, Rene's got one, Denise has one, there are several at the cutting horse farm.

Wait a minute! What's the difference between a bay and a chestnut? A bay has black legs and a black mane and tail. That's simple enough to change! If Denise ran into town for black hair dye, I could, at least temporarily, turn her into a blood bay.

Ten minutes later I slipped behind the tall blue spruce lining my driveway and quickly got her inside the barn. After I clipped her to the cross-ties I ran to the tack room and swung wide the cupboard door with emergency numbers taped inside. My fingers were slow and stiff with cold on the phone's keypad.

"Sheriff's Department," a feminine voice with a bored, nasal quality answered.

"Sheriff Morton, please."

"Not in on Saturdays. Can someone else help you, ma'am?"

I wanted the head honcho. "No, I need the sheriff." I knew the futility of asking my next question, but did it anyway. "May I have his home phone number?"

"It's against our policy to give out unlisted home numbers, but if it's an emergency, we can page him and relay a message."

Policy. How sick I was of that word. "Page him and tell him Carol Ward found what he's looking for. He'll know what I mean. Tell him I'm at home," I said. I rattled off my home address and phone number.

Next I dialed Denise.

"Denise?" Silence when she heard my voice. "You're probably still mad about yesterday, and we can talk about that later, but right now, this is an emergency and I need your help."

I jumped back in before she could interject anything. "Jack's truck wouldn't start this morning, so he took mine and I have no way to get to town. I need some black hair dye as soon as possible."

"Honestly, Carol, your hair doesn't look that bad. It could easily wait until your next appointment."

Just what did she mean by *that bad*?

"Whatever you do, don't go as dark as black, your complexion is much too fair."

"Denise…"

"Why don't you make an appointment with my sister? She's good with color."

"Denise!" I yelled into the phone to get her attention, "This isn't for me, it's for Feather."

"For Feather?" she asked incredulously. "It's illegal to change a horse's color and markings!"

"I don't have time to explain now, can you just trust me?" I asked.

"This better not be anything that'll get me barred from the Quarter Horse Association, because I swear to God, Carol Ward, if I have to forfeit the points Beezer and I've accumulated, I'll throttle you but good!"

She sounded like she meant it. "You won't be in trouble, I swear it!"

"Oh, all right. I don't know how I get sucked into these hare-brained ideas of yours. Revlon or Clairol? My sister says L'Oreal is…"

I cut her off. "I don't give a damn what brand!"

Her tone turned icy. "You know, Carol, when you're asking a favor, you could at least be polite. I'll get your stupid hair color as soon as I'm done watching my General Hospital tape. I'll be over in an hour or two." Click.

General Hospital! A crazed killer was combing the neighborhood looking for me, while Denise, no doubt sipping a Bloody Mary and smoking cigarettes, soaked up that tripe. She'll be sorry, if by the time she shows up, all she finds is my dead body. Let her explain that to Sheriff Morton.

Patiently standing on the cross-ties, Feather waited to be untacked and rubbed down. "You're a good horse; you saved my life," I said, hugging her. I pulled the tape recorder from the pocket, laid it on the fifty-gallon feed drum in the tack room and went back to Feather.

Using a circular motion, and a lot of elbow grease, the flexible plastic teeth of the currycomb unmatted dried sweat from her coat, then I went over her with a soft brush. When I finished, I put her in her stall, filled water buckets, and gave them each a flake of hay. I grabbed the recorder off the feed bin on the way out of the barn and minutes later unlocked the sliding glass door, letting myself into the house.

CHAPTER FOURTEEN

Afraid and alone in the house, I expected someone behind every door, leering at me from the shadows, even though I knew I hadn't been followed. The trembling fingers I ran through my hair pulled at the ends nervously. What were my options? I could call the police again, but what good would that do? Denise will be here soon, I told myself, and after that Jack will be home from work. And Sheriff Morton may be on his way this very minute. My practical side said the time spent waiting could be put to good use by listening to Julie's tape.

The cassette was damp with condensation, but otherwise seemed no worse for wear. Wiping it dry with a paper towel, I popped it into the tape player. I thought about waiting for Sheriff Morton, but the lure of the unknown was just too inviting. Not sure of what I might hear, and not even sure of what I *wanted* to hear, with more than a little trepidation, I pushed play. Above the scratchiness, with the volume turned up as high as it would go, were the sounds of any woodland, the melodious mixture of chirping and chatter that becomes white noise to the outdoorsman. I fast forwarded, stopping to listen at intervals, making sure I checked the first side entirely.

It contained nothing except what was supposed to be there: Birds. Sweet and peaceful, harmonious and pleasant. The cats gathered around, listening. Boots inquisitively batted one of the speakers, as if she expected it to fly away, then gave up, disgruntled. Camille tilted her head and stared into space.

No clues at all! Nothing! Downhearted, but also slightly relieved, I figured I might as well listen to the other side, too, just to make sure, so I ejected the tape and flipped it over. In an overstuffed easy chair that was much too comfortable, with a bag of Oreos, I had nearly dozed off, when abruptly the chirping stopped. I sat straight up, suddenly wide awake.

There was a rustling, like someone walking through tall grass. And whistling.

"You're late," came a man's voice, low and gravelly.

The room seemed to reverberate. I strained to decipher the words. "Here's three hundred, your cut from the diamond brooch and the emerald ring. They both sold last week."

The voice was familiar, but I couldn't place it. Low, gravelly, like someone with a sore throat. I thought of the places I typically go: the supermarket, feed store, library, the bank; and the people I see at those places, trying to match the voice. No connection.

"Three Hundred!" A second man spoke, and though I didn't recognize this voice, of one thing I was certain—neither of them were Derrick. "What about the other two diamonds and the opal ring? This is bullshit! You're holding out on me, you slimebag."

"First of all, one of your diamonds was a shit piece of zirconium." Haughty and authoritative, I sensed he was in charge, perhaps older. "It's not worth anything except the gold in the band. I'm still working on the other pieces. You'll have to wait. I can't design this stuff overnight. I've got to reset stones, change settings, make sure there aren't any inscriptions on the gold. And selling it takes even longer."

Diamonds and opals. Jewelry. My pulse throbbed in my temples; I felt my head would explode. Suddenly I was back in the woods again, instead of listening to a tape. I saw the gloved hand reach out, yanking Feather's rein from my grip. Of course, Julie's ring! The jeweler and my attacker were the same person. Someone supplied him with stolen jewelry, then he remade the pieces so they were indistinguishable from the original and sold them in his store, splitting the profit with the thief.

"How do I know you're telling the truth about what you've sold?"

"Trust me; you're making a lot more through me than you would through your pawn shop buddy." He snickered. "Surprised I know about your fence? Who's holding out on who?"

"What'd you think I did with the electronics?"

"There weren't supposed to be any electronics. The deal was you work for me, not yourself!"

"You don't own me! I'll sell anything to anybody, any time I feel like it. Ain't you or nobody else gonna' tell me I can't."

Camille nibbled the forgotten Oreo in my hand. I set it on the floor for her and got another from the bag.

"If you're smart, Boy Wonder, you'll keep this between us. The more people that know, the more chance we stand of getting caught. And in case you didn't notice, *we* includes you, too. You'll go down just like me."

"I ain't goin' down with nobody."

"We'll see about that. What'd you get last night?"

"A couple diamond rings and a purple bracelet."

"Amethyst?"

"How should I know? I'm not the expert. And a shitload of watches and a pearl necklace."

"Watches are useless. I told you not to bother with them; too easily identified."

"So throw 'em away. I grabbed the whole pile. It's not like I'm camping out at these houses, sortin' through stuff."

"Meet me here, week after next, same time. Lay low; maybe I'll sell something in the meantime."

"I can't live on this for two weeks! And don't tell me you ain't got more, because I saw your new Harley parked at the trailhead. All shiny black, not a speck of dirt on it. What'd you drop on that baby?"

"What I drive and what it costs are none of your business. Call the store Thursday. Some batty woman with blue fingernails came in this morning and liked the opal ring. Suckered her husband into putting a deposit down and said she'd be back next week with the rest."

"Thursday then."

"You leave first; I'll wait. I don't want anybody seeing us together."

For a short time the recording grew quiet, until I heard a snapping sound, like a branch or twig breaking.

"Who's there?" I heard him ask.

No one answered.

Now he demanded, "Who's there?"

A woman screamed.

"Stop!" he yelled.

Now the forest was eerily quiet, except for a sharp crack in the distance, singular and final, and afterward, nothing.

Each side of the tape was forty-five minutes long. I was near the end of this side, but kept listening, making sure there was nothing more on it. Minutes later I heard my own voice, and the unmistakable click-clack of horseshoes.

"Oh great, nail down everything that moves and board up your house," I said.

I tried to piece together what must have happened. Julie must have laid or sat in the tall grass that day, after planting the tape recorder. She probably tried to stay quiet so she wouldn't frighten the birds. Maybe she even slept in the warm sun. If she awoke when the two men showed up, but didn't move, she would have witnessed everything.

I imagined the panic she must have felt in trying not to give herself away, by not moving a muscle or daring make a sound. The indecision of whether to run or stay hidden. The gunshot in the distance told me she made a fatal mistake, and ran. That also explained why the tape recorder wasn't found closer to her body.

But the time elapsed between the jeweler calling out "Who's there?" and the gunshot was short. She was found in the Tamaracks, a good five minutes by horseback. She couldn't have run that far in that amount of time, so how did she end up in the pines?

"Why didn't you just stay put, Julie?" I said aloud. "A few minutes more and he would have been gone." Inside me was an emptiness, a dark, raw hole. Was this what it came down to, Julie's life in exchange for this? What a terrible waste.

A loud crack of thunder shook the house. In the time while I'd listened so intently to the tape, the sky had gone black, illuminated only by intermittent flashes of lightning on the horizon. Our little Russian Olive bush in the backyard was bent on its side, the wind stripping it of tiny white blossoms.

The phone crackled with static when I called the police station again. "Has anyone heard from Sheriff Morton?"

"Yes, ma'am, we did, and we gave him your message," said the woman with the stuffy nose. "He's on his way. Should be there any minute."

Time was running short; I couldn't wait any longer. The water tank in the paddock needed to be filled and hay thrown down before the electricity went out.

The cats were huddled behind the dryer, in one big furry jumble. I rummaged through my dresser drawers, throwing underwear and socks on the floor, then pulling out the purple scarf Jack got me for Christmas. A babushka, he called it. I folded it into a triangle and tied it under my chin. From Jack's side of the closet I wrenched an army surplus greatcoat from its hanger, for once glad he hadn't thrown something away. The sleeves hung below my hands, so I bunched them up at the elbows as best as I could. In the back of the closet I found old black rubber galoshes. Covered from head to toe, I didn't think I'd be recognized. I tucked the cassette into the pocket of the overcoat.

The fifty-gallon drum of sweet feed would make a good cache for the tape until it was safely in the hands of the sheriff. I set the heavy steel lid on my saddle. With the feed scoop, I dug into the sticky sweet grain mixture and put the tape into the small hole I'd burrowed, then covered it over.

Feather was in her stall, the one with the trap door overhead, so I'd have to push the outside door to the loft open, and drop the bales down, hurrying to carry them inside before the rain started. The long woolen flaps of the overcoat tangled around my legs, slowing my way up the creaky steps.

The locking hasp on the outside door was held shut by the sharp end of a hay hook slid through the ring. I pulled the hay hook out and wedged it into a crack between two boards. Brushing aside the cobwebs, I threw my shoulder against the door, but the old, moisture-swelled wood was stuck tight. Thunder rumbled again, reminding me I was wasting time, a precious commodity.

If I moved Feather out of her stall, onto the cross-ties, I could drop the hay through the hole in the floor, down into her stall, instead of using the outside door.

Jack's old motorcycle, cadaverous beneath a dusty tarp, stood tethered by cobwebs in a far corner of the loft. Shadows fell from the spokes, casting elongated dark lines across the stairway. I sucked in my breath and scooted down the stairs, two at a time, turning at the bottom to look back up.

There's nothing up there but spider webs, hay and old junk—no ghosts, I told myself.

Slipping Feather's soggy halter over her ears, I pulled her out of her stall and clipped her to the cross-ties, her soft brown eyes following me. I ran back up the narrow stairway. On the last step, the coat caught around my ankles, sending me sprawling. My knee banged hard on the edge of the step. Without a thought for the pain, I heaved two bales down the drop hole as fast as I could. When I stepped away from the trap door, lightning filled the loft. A single bare light bulb, dangling from the peak of the rafters, snapped and died, pitching me into darkness.

Suddenly the loft seemed claustrophobically close. I knew the opening in the floor was just behind me and to the left, but everything seemed to move between the strobe-light flashes, as I inched my way to the staircase, along the edge of the stacked hay. Gauzy nets of cobwebs caught in my hair, sticking to my eyes and lips. I spat and clawed, pulling them from my face.

Then I smelled cigarette smoke.

At once, both overjoyed and angry, I yelled, "Put that cigarette out, right now!" Denise should know better than to smoke in my barn. My eyes were slowly adjusting.

Suddenly a gush of air swept past me and a hand clamped my wrist in a crushing grip. A shiver shot through me and my heart jumped to my throat.

"Where is it?" he hissed, so close to my face I felt his warm breath on my skin and smelled the stale tobacco smell of his jacket.

I struggled against his hold, but my efforts were weak, like a child's futile wriggling in a parent's strong grasp. Cold sweat trickled down my back. Somehow he'd found me. With every brilliant illumination from the sky, I saw his face close to mine, his lips pulled back in an ugly grin.

"Where's what?" I croaked, trying my hardest to answer in a strong voice. Keep him talking, I told myself, buy some time.

"You know what I'm talking about!" he seethed. "You must have known I'd be here sooner or later, so where'd you hide it?"

"I don't know what you're talking about, and let go of me! Who are you anyway and what are you doing here?" I asked angrily.

Keep him talking.

"Don't play dumb with me. I saw you find that tape recorder in the woods. I was out there looking for it myself."

For some, playing dumb came naturally, or at least that's what Jack always said. "So take it! I don't want it. It's just a cheap cassette player."

"It's the tape I want, not the recorder."

"What for? It's only birds." Stall for time, play innocent.

"You could say I have a vested interest in it."

"It's up at the house. Let go of me and I'll get it."

"I've already been through your house. You really should lock your doors, you can't be too careful these days," he said sarcastically.

Never let your opponent see you sweat, my father's voice echoed. Keep him talking.

"How'd you find me?" I asked coolly.

"I recognized you from the other day at my store. All I had to do was go back and look up your address on the claim tag."

Of course, it was so simple.

"But even so, that gave you plenty of time to listen to the tape and hide it. It's not in the house, so it's either on you or somewhere in this barn."

He'd never find it unless I told him. *What are my choices here?* I asked myself. I couldn't break free of his grip, and even if I did, where would I go? He stood between me and the stairway, my escape route.

Help from the outside, Denise or Sheriff Morton, was my only hope. Why hadn't I called Jack? He would have been here by now. Wasn't he always there when I needed him?

Open a new avenue of conversation. This one's dead.

"You'll never find it; not in a million years, and that's just how long you're going to be in prison." Boldness disguised my panic. "Why'd you kill her? She would've been too scared to rat on you." My wrist ached where he held it.

He hesitated and for a moment, I feared I'd gone too far. "I never meant to kill her." In the dim light I saw a faraway look in his eyes. "I only wanted to talk to her, but she ran. It all happened so fast. The gun was in my hand and before I realized it, I'd shot her."

His back was to the stairwell. Looking behind him, over his shoulder, I saw a shadow move at the bottom of the stairs.

"At first I carried her; I was going to get help. But you and the other lady came up the trail; I panicked and I left her. I waited, thinking I'd come back later, but by dark, the park ranger was out."

"This is your chance to go to the police and tell them what you just told me. It wasn't exactly an accident, but it wasn't premeditated, either." Was he beyond reasoning?

"It's too late."

"There's no other way. Do you really think they won't catch up to you?"

A loud crack of thunder shook the barn so hard I flinched. Both horses whinnied; Feather's hooves clattered on the asphalt aisle. Rain finally kicked in, pounding against the roof and sides of the barn. The wind blew a fine spray up under the openings in the rafters and I felt it, cold and wet, on my face. Held in the hand by his side I saw a pistol, and I knew my life was assured only as long as I kept the tape hidden.

Was the sleepy kiss I'd given Jack this morning destined to be our last? Would I ever again tell him I loved him, that I'd always loved him, even through the bad times, when we fought, and when he was cranky and when the horses got into his garden and took bites out of his tomatoes and he yelled loud enough for the neighbors to hear?

When I yelled loud enough for the neighbors to hear?

It is said that in a crisis, your life passes before you. Mine played, silent and black and white, at warp speed, and in the end, it was reduced to one thing: Jack. An angry, stubborn resolve took hold of me. I simply would *not* die here, not now. There were too many words left unsaid, too many days not spent.

Lightning illuminated the stacked hay along the wall, and on the highest bale, I saw the glint of black diamonds in golden eyes, the devil's eyes. I saw the white encircling one side of his face, the white on his front paws and the white patch on his chest.

It was Hannibal, crouched low, ready to pounce. And, almost telepathically, I knew his silent plan, calculating his window of opportunity, the flawless moment, when he and I would align perfectly. I saw rippling muscles spring forward, sending the sinewy body catapulting through the air, curved fangs and razor-sharp claws ready for the moment they met the eyes and tender facial skin of my opponent. I saw bright red beads emerge and form thin rivers that ran down his face where Hannibal raked the flesh in rows as straight and symmetrical as a meticulously planted cornfield. He let go of my wrist, I spun around and, with one strong jerk, wrenched the hay hook free of the wall. With all my might, I slammed the piercing hook down hard, at the base of his neck.

CHAPTER FIFTEEN

We moved in a slow-motion time warp devoid of sound. I saw his mouth open but never heard him scream, then I saw the pistol he held come up to hit me square in the jaw. He fell sideways, against the unlatched hayloft door, the curve of the bloody hay hook still buried in his back. His weight unwedged the rain-soaked door and on rusty hinges, it flew open. The big diamond dinner ring he wore flashed when his hand twisted, his nails gouging splinters from the wooden door frame as he desperately clawed for a hold. Then the diamond ring slipped out of sight.

The door swung back and forth, creaking in the wind.

Sandbags weighed down my arms and legs. A cocoon of still, dark air enveloped me. If I closed my eyes, I could sink into the warmth of the cocoon forever, shedding my tiredness.

But someone told me to fight, don't give in, things aren't easy, Carol, he said. Life isn't easy. I heard his voice and I tried, for him, I tried, but it was too strong, so I surrendered and closed my eyes. "Just for a minute," I said. "I'm so tired. Please don't be angry."

"Carol, are you all right?" Denise asked.

The hayloft was foggy. Denise and Sheriff Morton crouched over me. Hannibal, perched on my stomach, bored unwavering golden eyes into mine. My head ached.

"What happened? Did he hit you? What was he doing in your hayloft, anyway?" Denise fired questions, one after another, like someone throwing darts.

Sluggishly forming words with deliberation, as if I'd drunk too much wine, I asked, "Did he get away?"

"Hardly," Sheriff Morton said, "I called for ambulances, but he's not going to need one."

If that was a riddle, I didn't get it. I touched my face, then looked at my hand to see if there was blood. There wasn't.

"Don't try to move," he said. "The medics will be here soon."

"No."

"No what?" he asked.

"No hospital," I said weakly. The fog was lifting.

Denise stood, her hands on her hips. "First of all, Carol Ward, we've already called EMS and they're on their way; secondly, you've been unconscious and shouldn't try to get up or move around."

My head hurt too bad to argue. I wanted to cry or swear or scream, or all three, anything to take away this pain. My left eyelid seemed to be closing over my eye.

"And third, but not least, why are you dressed like a bag lady?"

"Disguise." I felt sick to my stomach. "Feather's dye," I said.

"Now who died? One more person kicks the bucket in this town and that's it, I quit," Sheriff Morton said.

Denise turned to him. "Not dye like dead. Hair dye. For the horse."

"Who's Feather?" he asked.

"Oh my God, Denise, she's still tied up on the cross-ties!" I said. It was a cardinal sin to leave a horse unattended on the cross-ties.

"Somebody's tied up?" Sheriff Morton asked.

Lifting my head, my jaw throbbed, so I sank back down. "My horse," I said. If I laid absolutely still, the pounding stopped. "Where is he?"

"Where's who?" Denise asked.

"Mr. What's-his-name, the jewelry store man," I said.

"There's a guy under your hay drop, if that's who you mean," Denise announced matter-of-factly. "I was coming across the lawn when I heard a bloodcurdling scream from behind the barn, so I ran around back and there he was, his neck bent at an ungodly angle."

The sheriff's sagging jowls flopped when he spoke. "Broken neck."

"With a hay hook stuck in his back," Denise added.

"Dead?" I asked. Hannibal rubbed his face against mine.

"Afraid so."

A wave of nausea washed over me. I breathed in, counting to four, held it for a count of seven and exhaled to a count of eight. "I'm sick to death of dying," I said.

"So am I," Denise said. She pulled a pack of cigarettes from her pocket.

"Don't even think it," I warned.

"I'll be careful," she whined.

"No."

She scowled and put the cigarettes back.

"I was creeping up the stairs while you had him talking," Sheriff Morton said. "Heard the whole thing. We've got his cohort in custody. His statement, together with what I heard today, wraps it up. Did you find the tape?"

I nodded.

"Something told me you'd find it," he said.

"It's the snoop in her."

"Those damned overpaid detectives the county sent me wouldn't have found it if it grew legs and walked into the station."

"I listened to it after I left the message for you. Everything fits."

"What fits?" Denise asked.

"He admitted he killed her, but he didn't say why," Sheriff Morton added.

"Killed who?" Denise asked.

Between the three of us, it seemed we took turns being confused. "He killed Julie," I said. "She witnessed a meeting he had with his partner, the local cat burglar, who supplied him with stolen jewelry. He removed stones and changed settings to make the pieces indistinguishable from the original. He mixed the hot stuff in with the legitimate, sold it in his store, and split the profit."

The Sheriff stood and rocked back on his heels. "He, could, conceivably, have sold jewelry back to the very person it had been pilfered from without them realizing it. Quite a lucrative business."

"The thief wasn't making out too badly either," I said. Denise's head turned from side to side, as if she watched a tennis match. "He had a fence handling the electronics and guns and whatever else he got his hands on."

"We found a television with a number etched on it in a pawn shop. Turns out it matched the social security number of a burglarized homeowner. The fence knew we had him, so he gave us a description."

"Then how'd you find him?" Denise asked.

"The pawn broker said a kid brought it in, which narrowed our search considerably. All we had to do was plug the description into the computer, against juveniles with records, and there he was. Easy as pie." He laughed. "Truthfully, we got lucky. In today's high tech society, it still occasionally happens."

"But how'd you link him with the jeweler?" she asked.

"We didn't. We had no reason to believe he was working with anyone else, so we didn't tie the two together until now."

Sirens wailed. "Sounds like they're here," the sheriff said. "I'll get the gate."

Denise stayed with me while he went downstairs. A chain rattled and the front gate squeaked.

"I feel sleepy," I said.

"That's a symptom of a concussion," she said. "Or was it a skull fracture? I watched a program about head injuries on cable last week. Now that I think of it, it might have been a brain tumor."

"Thankfully, you're not a nurse."

"What's that supposed to mean?"

"Nothing."

"Are you suggesting my bedside manner is lacking?"

"Lacking? It's nonexistent."

The stairwell was a tight squeeze for the steel gurney brought up by two attendants. They prodded and pulled, lifted my arms and legs and flexed my joints and asked silly questions about relatives and would I spell my mother's maiden name. Then they lifted me onto the gurney and carried me down the stairs.

The light hurt my eyes where patches of blue broke through fast-moving gray. The storm was over. "Give the tape to the sheriff," I told Denise, shielding my eyes with my hand. "It's in the sweet feed drum."

She nodded. "How does your jaw feel?"

"Like hell. Is it black and blue?"

"Not now, but bruises always look worse later."

"Will you call Jack and tell him what happened? His work number is on the speed dial on the bedroom phone. Ask him to come to the hospital."

"Which one?"

"Mercy."

"The Catholic one?"

"Fishheads, Jack calls us." I squinted. "Give Hannibal a big hug for me."

"I'm not going anywhere near that nut case. When the sheriff and I found you, he was guarding you, sitting on your stomach and glaring at us with those weird yellow eyes."

"They're not weird, they're beautiful, like wolves' eyes," I said.

The other ambulance quietly drove across the lawn, toward the road. The sheriff came from behind the barn, stepping gingerly in the mud.

"Denise will get the tape," I told him.

"Don't worry yourself, Miss Carolyn, we'll take care of everything. Just get that old noggin checked out. I'll be calling the hospital in an hour or two to see how you're doing."

"Oh, look over there," Denise pointed. "In the back pasture. A rainbow." She squeezed my hand.

The sheriff winked and tapped the outside of the ambulance with his hand. The attendants closed the doors and I was off for my first, and hopefully last, ambulance ride.

CHAPTER SIXTEEN

"Stop pulling on his mouth! Let up on the reins!" Denise roared.

"I'm *not* pulling on his mouth; the reins are loose! They're flapping on his neck, they're so loose."

"Quit arguing or I'm not giving you any more riding lessons."

"This isn't like dressage at all. I don't like it."

"Shut up and ride. If you want to show in trail class, you've got to learn western."

It was Sunday, the day after all the hubbub and we were in my riding ring. I rode Echo in circles, around Denise. Her face was barely visible under the long visor of a baseball cap. Her untucked sleeveless shirt billowed in the breeze over tight jeans.

"With a curb bit, he feels the least little amount you pick up on the reins. You're confusing him because you're asking him to go forward and telling him to stop at the same time. Put your hands lower and in front of the saddle horn."

"Why can't I show him in a snaffle?" I whined.

"I already told you. It's against the rules, so don't ask again."

"Well, it doesn't make a bit of sense." Thrusting my hands awkwardly in front of me, my elbows weren't bent at all. This can't be right, I thought.

"And don't lean forward. Just because you're giving with the reins doesn't mean you lean forward."

I eased myself deeper into the saddle. "Can I stop for a minute? My jaw is throbbing."

The doctors told me I was fine, just a badly bruised jaw, no restrictions on activities, painkiller as needed, and pronounced me fit to send home. After what felt like an eternity of wearing their paisley-print cotton nightshirt with no back, I was more than ready to slip back into my bag lady attire. Sitting in a wheelchair in the hall, I was waiting to be discharged when Jack burst through the doors like a bull, his face ashen.

"What the hell happened?" he asked.

A woman in aqua scrubs glanced over. "Keep your voice down," I said, "I'll fill you in on the way home."

"Get dressed, and let's go."

"I am dressed."

His eyes traveled to the black rubber galoshes, their buckles dangling open. "What on earth possessed you to wear those?"

"I'll explain everything on the way home, I promise. It'll all make sense," I said, tucking the thick woolen coat around me.

"That'll be a first," he said sarcastically. "Nothing you've done so far has ever made sense, why start now?"

Denise's voice beckoned me from my daydream. "I'm sorry, I should've remembered your jaw and not drilled so hard. You and Echo will get it eventually, you'll see, and all of a sudden, it'll be like a light bulb flicked on."

A car door slammed. It wasn't Jack, I knew, because he was up in the house enjoying a day off, although I can't say I understand someone who chooses to spend a gloriously sunny late-April day on the sofa, watching reruns.

Kathy waved. In hunter green slacks and shirt with the park ranger patch sewn on the shoulder, she easily shimmied between the oak fence boards.

"I'd be stuck like a cow if I tried to wedge myself between those boards," Denise laughed. "You'd have to pry me out with a crowbar!"

"For crying out loud, Denise, we wouldn't either. But I'm glad to see you two getting along better," I said.

"Oh, speaking of that," Kathy said, "I talked to the head honcho in Lansing. They aren't spraying for the moths west of Blood Road, so you're more than safe."

Denise looked down, gouging the toe of her boot into the sand and saying nothing.

"Anyway," Kathy continued, "I've got more good news."

"We can always use that," I said.

"Derrick's decided he wants to be a park ranger. He'll have to get a GED and then an associate's degree, but he's willing to put in the time and effort. He can live with me and commute to college in Flint."

"You must be thrilled," I said.

"I'm ecstatic. For the first time, he's actually got a goal, something to work toward."

There was the softness of a mother's love in her sparkling eyes. "Last night, when everything was over, we sat down and talked about a lot of things. I guess I'd put off asking any questions, afraid of what the answers might be." She squinted in the bright sun. "And he wasn't exactly truthful with you, Carol, when you found him way out by that old stone wall."

"His story sounded fabricated at the time," I said, "that's why I had my doubts."

Denise threw me a warning glance. "Not that anyone for an instant thought he was mixed up with Julie's murder," she quickly added.

"Absolutely not," I said, pulling imaginary hay wisps from Echo's mane.

Kathy laughed. "You'll never guess what he was really doing, and he'd kill me if he knew I told you. He was picking flowers."

"Picking flowers?" I asked incredulously.

"Teenage boys have this thing about hiding behind a macho front," she said. "They're afraid someone will see the real person underneath. My separation from his father hasn't helped either. Or living in the heart of Detroit, where just staying alive takes up all your time."

"Actually, maybe that's what helped him see what's really important," I said.

"You may be right. Why his dad chooses to live there, I'll never understand," she said.

"City people don't understand why we want to live out here," Denise said. "Chores from sunup to sundown, mowing and gardening, mucking stalls, putting up hay, it's endless. They want condo associations and lawn specialists and the snow shoveled from their walk before they get up in the morning."

"I suppose," I agreed, glancing around me. The fence needed painting, the barn roof was beginning to sag, and lawn mowing was continual from April through October. "But I wouldn't give it up. When I see the morning mist lifting from my horses' backs, and the tree line in the back is all gold and coral and amber, then I remember why I'm here."

"The horses, that's it for me," Denise said. "If I had to ride in an arena every day, I'd rather not ride at all."

"Horses!" Kathy said, "I almost forgot the reason I stopped over—Rene needs homes for her horses."

"She's not keeping them?" I asked.

"It looks like her and Ron might get back together."

"That's great," Denise said. "But what's that got to do with the horses?"

"Rene's talking about going to California with Ron, instead of him moving back here. He's got a great job and teachers are needed everywhere, so it's not as if Rene won't be able to find something out there. But even so, I hate to see her go."

"Good teachers are a dying breed," I said.

"She never really had all that much interest in riding; it was mostly Julie," Kathy said. "She asked me if I'd take one of the horses and I told her I would, especially since Derrick's going to be staying. Denise, I know your old Arabian can't be ridden anymore and I told her you might be interested. One's a buckskin, and one's a bay. I think she's willing to give them away, to good homes."

Denise's face lit up. "I'd love to have either one." Then she sheepishly added, "I've always wanted a buckskin."

"I'll take the bay," Kathy said. "When she calls, act surprised; don't let on that I already told you."

Echo had nodded off. His head was lowered, almost to the ground, and his lip was drooping. But he came to immediate attention, along with Kathy, Denise and I, when the now-familiar black and white patrol car pulled into the drive.

Sheriff Morton was neatly dressed in his starched brown uniform, paunchy middle protruding slightly over the top of his belt. He wore his holster and gun and looked very official despite the half-eaten ice cream cone he munched on. Every trace of mud was gone from his spit-shined shoes.

"Afternoon, ladies." He turned to me. "And just what do you think you're doing up there on that horse? If I remember correctly, you spent yesterday afternoon in the hospital after being knocked unconscious. I'd be mighty obliged if you'd get down off that horse and take it easy for a few days. We've had enough excitement around here—ambulances running all up and down these back roads like there was a war going on. Did the doctors say it was okay for you to be horseback riding and all this here kind of nonsense?"

I felt red creeping up my neck and into my face. "Actually," I said, "the doctor said normal activities were fine, and for me, sitting on a horse is a normal activity."

"We only did walk and trot," Denise added. "Any moron should be able to do that."

Had I just been insulted? "Why's everybody staring at me?" I asked.

"I rest my case," the sheriff said.

"There's one thing I can't figure out," Denise said. "If Carol and I were so close when he killed Julie, why didn't we hear the gunshot? How could we have missed it?"

"You were probably still on the road or just riding into the tall pines when he shot her. Where Carol found the tape, in the oak tree with the owl's nest, it's hilly, dense forest. Hills and foliage absorb sound. And you both told me you were chatting and not really paying attention to your surroundings, which would make sense, since you had no reason to do otherwise. I'm not surprised you heard nothing."

"I just keep wondering if we'd noticed or heard something, we might have had a chance to save her," I said.

"Yeah," Denise agreed.

But the sheriff shook his head. "You could've gotten yourselves killed to boot. He murdered once, why wouldn't he do it again? Besides, from what the experts tell me, she was beyond help almost instantly."

"Does this mean our woods are safe again?" Denise asked.

"Except for the despondent, cocaine-using lost husband," I reminded her. A knock on the jaw hadn't affected my memory.

"Some mushroom hunters found him yesterday, propped up against a tree over by the lake," the sheriff said. "Nearly dead from hypothermia. Easy enough to get with all the cold, wet weather we've had, especially someone as skinny as him, probably didn't have an ounce of body fat."

"I should be so lucky," I said. "Not to have an ounce of body fat, I mean, not hypothermia."

"When he's released from the hospital, he's headed straight to drug rehab." He popped the last of his ice cream cone in his mouth and wiped his fingers on a monogrammed handkerchief pulled from his shirt pocket. "I've got to be running along. You girls have a nice afternoon. And, if you can, try to keep things calm and quiet in this neighborhood for awhile, okay? The past two weekends have been hell."

Kathy laughed. "You'll never again hear me complain about the boredom of a park ranger's job!"

Denise's hand rested on the crest of Echo's neck. "Speaking of running along, I'd better do the same. It's beef Stroganoff tonight. The meat's been marinating in wine since last night. Should be ninety proof by now."

"Your meals always sound so wonderful, so exquisite, so...," I searched for the word, "so gourmet."

"There's a thing called a cookbook, Carol, get yourself one. It'll change your life."

CHAPTER SEVENTEEN

Jack sat on the couch, a can of beer in one hand and a fried chicken leg in the other, fully engrossed in the car race.

"Jack?" I asked.

"Yeah?" His head might have turned a fraction of an inch, but his eyes stayed glued to the television.

"I'm taking Hannibal to a cat psychiatrist next month." The poor little guy needed it more than ever now, after the harrowing experience he'd been through.

"That's nice," Jack mumbled.

Be vague about the cost, I told myself. "It's not real expensive, but it's not cheap, either."

"Sure, hon, whatever you say."

"Just thought I'd let you know." Next month, when he balanced the checkbook and asked why I wrote a check for an as yet undisclosed amount to a Dr. Baker, D.V.M., I would noncommittally say, "Don't you remember, dear? I told you I was taking Hannibal to a kitty psychiatrist. You said it was a nice idea."

Then I could go into my rendition of how he never listens to a thing I say. In one ear and right out the other.

I smelled a guilt complex brewing.

ABOUT THE AUTHOR

Karen Wilson has experience in both the worlds of journalism and horses. She has written for two newspapers and has ridden and shown horses both in hunt seat and dressage.

She lives in Southeastern Michigan with her husband, ten cats and two horses. She enjoys watercolor painting, cross-country skiing and riding, but regrettably has been unable to squeeze in time for the accordion lessons suggested by her husband.

Printed in the United States
951100004B